A KEEPER'S TALE

THE STORY OF TOMKIN AND THE DRAGON

JA ANDREWS

For my husband.
I love you.

A KEEPER'S TALE

THE FAMILIAR INN smelled of roasted apples, spiced with possibilities. Lulu threaded her way among hips and legs, stepping over fancy, clean townsfolk shoes and muddy, worn farmer boots. She ducked under elbows and slipped through the hum of anticipation, until she caught a glimpse of the black robe next to the hearth. She shouldered past the last of the crowd and felt the fire warm her cheek.

There really was a Keeper, settled in a chair only steps away, in merry conversation with the baker and the blacksmith.

Lulu paused. Weren't Keepers supposed to be white haired and hunched? This man's hair was as black as his robe. He wasn't what she was expecting, and she almost ducked back into the crowd. It was his eyes that stopped her. They weren't serious or weighty. They were bright, and he glanced around the room with a curiosity Lulu understood. When he glanced down at her, his eyes crinkled around the edges.

"Hello." He smiled. "I'm Will."

Lulu smiled back, hesitantly at first, but it was impossible for her to hold in smiles on a normal day, never mind on a night when a Keeper came to town.

1

"Hello," she said, grinning. "I'm Lulu." She wanted to say more, to ask him…but he was a Keeper, and the familiar room had turned into an enormous cavern with the townsfolk crowded behind her like giants.

The Keeper leaned forward. "You look like a young lady with a question."

Lulu's heart skipped. She had a thousand questions. But tonight only one mattered. She leaned forward as well, gathering her courage.

"Can you do magic?" she whispered.

Will's eyebrows rose. "Oh," he said in a quiet, serious voice—a Keeper sort of voice, "Keepers have far more serious things to do than perform magic tricks for little girls covered in grass." He plucked a little green stalk out of her hair.

Lulu sank back and bit her lip. It was so very hard to keep clean.

But Keeper Will held it out toward her with the tiniest hint of a smile. Before she could reach for it, the little snip of green stretched and the end of it swelled, until tiny white flowers burst out of it.

Lulu's heart burst open with it. Magic! He had done magic! She took the flower in awe.

"Tonight," the Keeper continued, "I am here to do something better. Tonight I'm telling stories."

Lulu rolled the little flower stem between her fingers. It was the most amazing thing she'd ever seen. "Why bother telling stories when you can do magic?"

He laughed. It was that sort of laugh grownups do, not because they think it's funny, but because they've been caught off guard.

"You ask all the right questions, my dear." He studied her for a moment. "The sort of questions a Keeper might ask."

Lulu's pulse quickened.

"How old are you?"

"Seven."

"Ahh." Will sat back in his chair. "Then it will be a few years before we know if you are a Keeper or not. If, in a couple years, you do anything—" He waved his fingers through the air. "—magical, come to Queenstown and find the Court Keeper. We've been waiting a very long time for a new Keeper, you know."

Lulu beamed at him. "My mother says I have more questions than a Keeper."

The man threw back his head and laughed again, the sound filling the room. It was loud enough that the room gave the Keeper their attention and shuffled to find seats.

Keeper Will bent close to her again and whispered, "I haven't answered your question yet." His voice carried throughout the room when he continued, "Keepers tell stories, because stories are the most powerful thing on earth. A good story can wiggle its way into the deepest part of your heart. It can shape your dreams or your fears. It can change how you see the world. It can even change—" He tapped her nose with his finger. "—how you see yourself.

"And *that* is real magic."

Lulu glanced down at the flower in her fingers.

"Lulu is unconvinced," he said to the room. "So I'll attempt to prove it." He turned back to her. "Is there a story you'd like to hear?"

"Tomkin and the Dragon," she blurted out, almost before he was done asking. A round of hollers and cheers agreed with her.

The Keeper leaned back and nodded. "That's the exact sort of story I'm talking about. Excellent choice, Lulu."

He pulled his hood up and stared down at the floor for a long moment, perfectly still. The room sank down into silence, and Keeper Will began.

PART I

Tomkin Thornhewn,
youngest son of the Duke of Marshwell
and aspiring hero,
slipped at the very worst moment.

-From Keeper Alaric's retelling
of Tomkin and the Dragon

CHAPTER ONE

ALONG THE SOUTHERN BORDER, a company of soldiers surged forward like the waters of the Great River, battling a deadly foe and performing acts of heroism.

At his desk, Tomkin Thornhewn sat still like the waters of a small puddle, shuffling through a pile of paper and only dreaming of such renown.

Beyond the door of Tomkin's small study, late summer sunlight streamed into the empty hall of Marshwell Holding. The only noise was the rustle of paper as Tomkin rummaged through curious old maps, stiff accounting pages, and the soldiers' skirmish reports, finally finding the letter from his father.

Tomkin,

Your brother, Elton, had a day worthy of one of your stories. While leading a morning patrol, he stopped to help a soldier whose horse had foundered, and discovered a stash of letters beneath the man's saddle. The soldier had been spying for Baylon the entire summer. 'Tis no wonder all our plans have failed. He confessed that the vile Baylonians hold his wife, who is with child. The poor woman is in the warlord's camp. She is kept in a cell, shackled.

Tonight, at dark, we infiltrate and rescue her from the devils. Would that I had an army instead of this small company! I would make sure the fiends did not survive the night. As it stands, we will trust to a moonless night and stealth.

When your mother returns from the north, the two of you should celebrate. Your plan for crossing the twin rivers was flawless. We at the front would have a hard time without minds such as yours supporting us from home.

With my love and gratitude,

Your father

Post note: I forgot to mention that Elton, while bringing the spy back to camp, heard a clink in the woods. When he investigated, he flushed out a scouting party from Baylon and captured their commander. The man is the highest-ranking prisoner we have ever caught. Heroics come more naturally to your brother than any man deserves. When he is duke, he shall do more between his first full moons than I have done in my entire life.

Tomkin shook his head and let out a huff somewhere between a laugh and a sigh. It would probably only take Elton a fortnight. He jotted down some notes on the soldiers' reports, putting them in order, underlining parts he'd add to Marshwell's official records.

...Sir Elton leapt from the rocks and knocked the Baylonese soldier from his horse...unhorsed two more devils with a single stroke. Tomkin underlined the phrase. How does one even do that?

Tomkin glanced out the window. It was past noon. Today's messenger should arrive soon with word from the border. How had his father's small band rescued a woman from a camp as large as the warlord's? There was a twinge of dread in his stomach. Or maybe it was hope. Or a stomach-churning combination of the two.

He imagined the captured woman cowering in the corner of an earthen cell. The soldiers moving through the woods, shadows slipping among the snakes of campfire smoke, the mouse-like creak of the cell door. Lifting the woman from the darkness, carrying her into the wide night.

The hall door swung open, scattering Tomkin's thoughts like a startled flock of birds, and he was back at his desk in Marshwell. Twinkles of dust spun lazily near the windows. The scent of roasting chestnuts wafted by.

"Dorlow the Candlemaker," the page announced.

Tomkin let out a long, deflated breath. Candles. Right. The holding needed candles. He gathered the soldiers' reports and closed them in his record book, setting it off to the side to make room for the accounting ledger.

"Send him in." Tomkin took a deep breath and straightened his shoulders. He could make his own day sound exciting. His brother might be off rescuing the helpless, but Tomkin was…buying candles…bringing light to the holding. Tomkin Thornhewn, Bringer of Light.

The stories from the army called to him, so Tomkin set a map facedown on the pile, hiding anything exciting from his view.

There was a shuffle of feet near the door to his study and Tomkin gave the candlemaker a short nod before opening his ledger and lifting his quill. "Good afternoon, sir. Your visit is timely. The holding is running low on candles." He glanced back at the records. "The price for a season's worth is ninety silver?" He looked up.

The fact that Dorlow was a candlemaker was so perfect, it almost made up for the fact he wasn't a maiden in need of rescue. The man looked like he had been made of wax, then hung to dry and stretch until everything, from his eyes to his jowls to his fingers, were long and droopy. He hung back by the door of Tomkin's study, wringing his hands, his fingers sliding and bending through each other in a way both mesmerizing and ghastly.

"Is there something wrong, sir?"

"M'lord." The man bobbed a short bow. "I'm afraid the price is not the same as last spring. You see, m'lord, there was a great fire in the forest near my home…"

Tomkin nodded. "We know of the fire. We were told no homes were damaged."

"No, sir, no homes. But the smoke, you see, sir, the smoke o' the fire settled down in the vale. All the bees, in all the hollows, fled." He clenched his hands together, his eyes anxious. "This is the last o' my supply o' candles, sir. I'm afraid I must raise my prices…" Dorlow's gaze dropped to his hands. "…to a hundred fifty silver."

Tomkin sat back. His mother was still annoyed he'd paid extra for that herd of cattle last month, even though the two bulls were bound to end up being worth the price. If he made another overly generous deal, she'd stick her nose back into his accounting. It had taken until his twentieth birthday to get her to leave it in his hands. He wasn't going to ruin it before a full season had passed. Especially over candles.

The candlemaker stepped forward. "I know ya think that's too high, sir. But I've searched the countryside. There aren't no bees. I'll need to travel to Southshire, or maybe as far as Greentree to find some." He paused. "I can't sell the candles to the common folk for the price I need, but I thought maybe you, sir, here at the holding…"

Tomkin tapped his quill on the paper. The candlemaker's asking price was obscene. But Dorlow made the only decent candles in the area, and the holding was running low. The scales in this particular deal were tipped in Dorlow's favor. His mind ran over the situation again. There was always a way to tip the scales. The holding needed candles. But what did a bee-less candlemaker need?

Tomkin bit back a smile at the most obvious question he'd ever asked himself. "My mother's gardens have a problem. Instead of the normal number of bees, which she insists are good for her plants—"

"Oh, they are, sir," Dorlow interrupted. "Bees'd be the reason her garden is so lovely. I saw one." He leaned forward. "The duchess has southern mint bees! They make rich, dark honey. And their tongues—" He raised one eyebrow for emphasis. "—are unusually long."

Tomkin tried not to grimace.

Dorlow settled back on his heels. "Real beauties, those mints."

Tomkin felt the scales begin to shift. "Recently a second hive has formed and the far corner of the garden is overrun with bees." He had been putting off dealing with the bee problem every day since his mother had left. "If you, sir, were willing to remove one of the hives, my mother would be deeply grateful. The bees would be yours to keep."

The candlemaker's entire face lifted at the news. "A hive o' long-tongued mints! Thank ya, sir! 'Tis a kingly gift!" He bent into a droopy bow. "Kingly!"

The scales clinked down on Tomkin's side. "Not a gift. Consider it partial payment. Ninety silver plus a hive of southern mint bees."

"Agreed!" Dorlow rubbed his waxy fingers together so quickly Tomkin was afraid they might catch fire.

The candlemaker hurried off, and Tomkin added a note to the list of things to tell his mother when she returned tomorrow.

...*The candlemaker skipped away to remove the hive and our intrepid hero relaxed after a battle well fought, pleased the holding would be lit with the glow of candles and the gardens would have fewer long-tongued beasts.* Tomkin finished with a flourish, smiling at the smooth line. Few things in life were more satisfying than writing with a good quill.

Life was one story after another. Some stories just needed a little help to make them interesting.

If Marshwell were an important duchy, or close to any important part of the world, the problems people brought to him might provide good stories all on their own. Tales of pirates or monsters or evil wizards. But instead, Marshwell was tucked away on the southern border of Queensland, and though it was one of the largest duchies, it was filled with peaceful hills and homey folk. Not far enough south to have exotic seas. Not far enough north to have perilous mountains. It was the sort of place a hero might pass through on a great quest, but only to find a safe night's rest in a comfortable barn.

Tomkin picked the map up off the pile of soldiers' reports and tilted it toward the window. He squinted to read the faded, spidery writing. The map showed a large, bean-shaped island in the Southern Sea. The isle was nameless besides the notation "Territory of Marshwell."

The sheer oddness of the map was pleasing. How did Marshwell, with the entire country of Coastal Baylon between it and the sea, own an island? Of course, the island was fairly Marshwellian: one lone volcano, surrounded by an unbroken expanse of grassy plains, and inhabited exclusively by a breed of hairless sheep.

What was the point of hairless sheep? If there was ever a place in need of a good story, it was this one. Tomkin let the map fall to the desk. It was a shame it wasn't a good island. One with sinister ruins. Or maybe an ogre. That would be better than the Isle of Bald Sheep.

The door to the hall opened. "A messenger from the Duchy of Greentree," announced the page.

A man with a squinty sort of face, pale skin, and lips thin as knife blades stepped in. He wore a green vest emblazoned with a silver tree.

"Good morning," Tomkin said, nodding politely. He

couldn't remember the last time they'd had correspondence from Greentree.

The messenger looked around the room, as though searching for a more suitable person to address, before offering Tomkin a slight bow. "The Lord of Greentree sends his personal reply to the Duke of Marshwell." The messenger glanced around again.

"The duke is my father," Tomkin said, holding his hand out.

The messenger, with obvious reluctance, held out a letter sealed with bright green wax and stamped with a tree. The man looked like a villain. Not a diabolical one—just the sort of minor henchman who delighted in piling discomfort and delays upon the hero. And probably enough paperwork to drown him.

Tomkin took the letter and considered it for a moment. It was addressed to his father, but the duke was at the border. And Tomkin's mother wouldn't be back until tomorrow.

He slipped his fingernail under the edge of the seal. "Is the letter urgent?"

The man's lipless mouth drew down into a frown. "I do not know." He sniffed. "I do not read letters not addressed to me."

The man was definitely a villain. But heroes didn't ignore their duty just because a minor foe disapproved. Tomkin gave the man a sour smile and broke the seal. He unfolded the letter, and his attention snagged on his own name.

Duke Thornhewn,

I have considered your proposal and agree a marriage between your son Tomkin and my daughter Lissa would be mutually beneficial.

. . .

Tomkin's mind slammed into the words and reeled back.

Lissa of Greentree? He was betrothed to Dragon-Lady Lissa?

No one had mentioned him marrying anyone, never mind a girl whose temper was legendary.

I agree the escalations from Coastal Baylon are troubling, and a united front on our side would serve to give them pause.

Lissa is a flame of joy in my life, even more so after our family's recent tragedy.

Flame of joy? By all accounts, she was a terror. Tomkin had never had the misfortune to meet her, but her reputation was enough. Rumor was her servants were terrified of her, and even Princess Ellona hated her. Tomkin couldn't remember exactly why, but he was sure it was true. Everyone said so.

Tomkin had seen Princess Ellona once, from a distance, when he had gone to Queenstown with his mother. She looked the way he'd always imagined an elf might: like a sparkle of light, even amongst the glitter of the court.

His father needed to find him a bride like the princess. Not Lissa.

I have heard of your son's quick mind. It is an honor to him, and to yourself, that he is able to carry so much responsibility in your holding.

As our children are of similar ages, I believe they have as fair a chance at happiness as any of us do. May their marriage be as companionable and fulfilling as yours, and as the one I enjoyed for so many years.

Yours in hope of a long and beneficial partnership,
Lord Norton of Greentree

• • •

Companionable and fulfilling?

No.

No, no, no.

Marriage to a girl as unpleasant as Lissa of Greentree would be torture.

The messenger cleared his throat. Tomkin looked up and caught a smirk before the man tucked it away into his weedy face. Villain.

"Marshwell does not have an answer for Lord Norton today," Tomkin said curtly.

The messenger bowed and left. Tomkin glared at his back until the door shut behind him.

"But we will have an answer." Tomkin glowered at the door. His voice echoed back, weak and petulant. Tomkin tapped his quill against the letter.

If his father were set on a match with Greentree, let Elton marry Lissa.

His father wouldn't do that, though. The truth was, if the duke was interested in an alliance with a duchy no more important than Marshwell, Tomkin was the obvious choice. Because Tomkin was the least valuable.

Something in his chest shriveled a little. It was true, of course. Elton had earned fame in battles with Coastal Baylon. Tomkin, younger, smaller and untrained in combat, was left to trade bees for candles. But that was hardly Tomkin's fault. If his father, brother, or any of the fighting men had been around for most of Tomkin's life, someone would have taught him to fight and he'd be on the border with the soldiers, claiming victory and glory.

Still, he had to be worth more than this.

Tomkin tapped his quill harder on the paper. He'd just prove he was valuable enough to marry anyone—even Princess Ellona herself.

With a sharp crack, the tip of Tomkin's favorite quill broke off. A droplet of ink slid out of the jagged end, spreading into a large, black blot. Tomkin let the ruined quill fall onto the letter and dropped his head into his hands.

Bees and candles weren't going to win him glory. There was nothing heroic about negotiating. He needed something big, something worthy of a story. He needed something even his fearless brother had never done. He needed something—

The door burst open and Tomkin's head snapped up. A huge, wide-eyed man rushed.

"Dragon!" the man gasped. *"Dragon!"*

A claw of fear clamped down on Tomkin's heart at the man's stark terror.

Well...yes, a small voice in his head said, *something like a dragon.*

CHAPTER TWO

A DRAGON IN MARSHWELL!

Tomkin's heart felt as if it was galloping out of his chest. He shoved his chair back and raced to the window searching for smoke and chaos. He saw nothing but blue sky.

"Not here, m'lord." The man grabbed his wool hat off his head and clutched it to his chest. "It was across the river, this very mornin', just as the sun comed up. A dragon flied down an' grabbed one of me li'l lambs—right off the grasses where it were grazin'!"

"A *dragon*?" Tomkin ran back to his desk and shoved papers aside looking for another quill.

The man bobbed a fast, twitchy nod. "Throwed the lamb down, blowed fire on it until it was all charred and cooked, then et it up!"

Tomkin paused. "It...cooked the sheep?"

The man nodded, wide-eyed.

Tomkin took a moment to look the man over. He was almost as big as the doorway behind him, with a grimy face and a neatly patched shirt. But if Tomkin set aside the man's size, it was easier to see he had a soft, simple look about him.

Not too old, but not young enough for the innocence in his expression.

The man's face was like one of the small children who tumbled about the holding, bringing their tales to Tomkin. Sagas of great battles fought behind the smithy, or the water demon they'd chased from the well. Stories of wildness and whimsy. Stories Tomkin wished were true. He had an entire book dedicated to their tales, a leather-bound volume sitting in a place of honor at the front corner of his desk.

"I see." Tomkin sank into his chair while his heart settled back into its usual place in his chest and reined in to a walk. He let his eyes run over the childlike man in front of him. He stifled a sigh that was part relief, part disappointment. There were no dragons in Marshwell.

Smiling kindly at the man, he reached to the front corner of his desk, picked up the leather-bound book, and flipped to a new page. "What is your name, sir?"

"Gerrold, m'lord." He gave a quick, awkward bow, never taking his frightened eyes off Tomkin.

Tomkin dipped the quill in some ink. "Please tell me everything that happened, Gerrold."

With much wringing of his hat, Gerrold repeated, three times, the very short story he had already told. Tomkin wrote it down, word for fantastical word.

"How big was the dragon?"

Gerrold spread his arms wide. "Dragon-sized."

"As it should be," Tomkin answered him seriously. "What did it look like?"

"Bright." Gerrold swallowed hard. "Bright as death."

Tomkin raised an eyebrow and gave the man an approving nod. That was a phrase worth keeping. "And the dragon took a small sheep, cooked it, ate it, and then flew off."

"Yes sir...into Colbreth Castle, sir."

Tomkin liked Gerrold more every moment.

Colbreth Castle. The only place in Marshwell that had ever been home to a dragon. Tomkin could think of no better place to imagine such a beast.

"The hill my sheeps graze on—" Gerrold dropped his gaze to the floor. "—well what's left o' my sheeps now, is across the river from the ruins o' the castle, so I seen it clear. That's where the dragon went."

"It's a fitting place."

"Yessir," Gerrold nodded. "My granpap was grazin' sheeps when the last dragon was there. From our hills, he saw the whole battle."

Tomkin set his quill down. "I would have loved to have seen that." He motioned for Gerrold to follow him into the hall. "There's the sword my Granduncle Horace used to fight that dragon."

Above the mantle, Scalebreaker sat on two large pegs, its blade made of plain steel, its ridged hilt unremarkable except for the fire-orange garnet nestled in the pommel. A flash of flame-colored light darted through the gem. There was something defiant in how it hung there.

Gerrold looked at the sword with the unreserved wonder Tomkin felt the blade deserved. An idea struck Tomkin. He probably shouldn't, but he couldn't pin down exactly why not. Another glance at Gerrold's awed face gave him the courage to do the thing he'd always dreamed of. Something he'd seen his father do only once, on a fire-lit night when a bard had filled the hall with words of glory and valor.

Tomkin stepped onto the hearth, stretched up, and wrapped his hand around Scalebreaker's hilt. The cold metal was fierce beneath his fingers. He lifted the sword. The blade slid off its peg and the tip plummeted, like a dragon plunging toward a lamb, until it clanked onto the floor. Gerrold's mouth hung open in astonishment.

That hadn't gone as smoothly as he'd imagined. Tomkin gave Gerrold a weak smile. "Would you like to hold it?"

The shepherd shook his head and clasped his hands behind his back. "No, sir." He cast a worried look at Tomkin's hand on the hilt. "Mama says I shouldn't play with sharp things."

"Ah, yes. Very wise." Tomkin shifted his hand on the hilt. So much for acts of kindness. Deciding he'd rather heave the heavy sword back onto the wall without an audience, Tomkin clinked it into the corner by the mantle.

He went back to his desk and jotted a note. "Gerrold, I appreciate that you brought this news to us so quickly, even though you must be very upset over the—" He couldn't say 'roasting.' "—the loss of your sheep. As a token of our gratitude, please take this note to the master of the sheep pens. He will help you to pick out a suitable replacement for the lamb that was taken."

The shepherd's face lit up and he bowed again, awkward and bobbing. His smile was too pure for a grown man's face —which reflected well on Gerrold, and poorly on the rest of the world. Tomkin gave the giant a short bow in return and watched him leave. He turned back to his book. Gerrold's story was so quirky and foreboding, it didn't need to be changed at all.

The only thing that would make it better, was if it were true.

What had Gerrold seen that had frightened him so much? It wasn't a dragon, that much was certain. Dragons weren't known for taking the time to roast their meals. Devouring, shattering, laying waste? Yes. Cooking? No.

Besides, dragons didn't come to Marshwell. There had been the one in his grandfather's time. But, though it had done a fair amount of damage to several villages, the truth was it had been older, with a large scar on its side where it was missing scales. Marshwell's only dragon had been elderly and defective.

Gerrold had probably seen a copper eagle. An eagle was

large enough to lift a lamb, and in the morning sunlight their coppery feathers would have shone bright enough for child-like Gerrold to have mistaken it for fire. His imagination would have filled in the rest.

Just seeing Colbreth Castle would be enough to make anyone imagine dragons. Years ago Tomkin's family had traveled south down the Great River. He could still picture the moment the boat had rounded the bend—there were the crumbling ruins of Colbreth Castle, perched halfway up a white cliff.

It was a shame Gerrold's story didn't need to be investigated.

Tomkin sighed, setting the story of the dragon aside, frowning at the uneven strokes the new quill had made.

He had seen a copper eagle quill once, glowing like molten iron in the candlelight. Copper eagles were rare. If there really was one at Colbreth Castle, a quill made from one of those feathers would be…

Maybe there was a reason to investigate after all.

Tomkin glanced out the window. There was no one left waiting to see him. With his mother and most of the staff gone there was barely anyone in the holding at all. It would be better than sitting around brooding about his impending marriage sentence.

Tomkin stepped out of his office into the empty hall and locked the door behind him. A glint of flame from the corner caught his eye, the sunlight flashing in the garnet on Horace's sword. Tomkin walked to it and wrapped his hands around the hilt, lifting the blade so it caught the light. The heavy sword felt as though it could slice though the stone floor. It felt inexorable.

"Are you going to fight the dragon?"

Tomkin spun, pointing the tip at the large form of Gerrold, who stood in the doorway clutching a lamb to his chest. Gerrold gazed at him with such eagerness, such admiration,

Tomkin straightened his shoulders. To someone like Gerrold, that was probably what this looked like. Tomkin was wearing his black tunic with the yellow and green shield of Marshwell on the sleeve. It wasn't too different from the uniforms the soldiers wore under their armor.

Unfortunately, it was impossible to fight an imaginary dragon. Not that he could say that to Gerrold. "I...I was just about to go check it out."

The giant man looked at the sword, speaking in a hushed, awed voice. "You're takin' Scalebreaker!"

Tomkin hesitated. He'd been nervous taking it off the wall. The idea of taking it out of the hall was terrifying. He glanced at the sword. Either terrifying or thrilling.

Gerrold beamed at him. "I didn' realize how much of a hero you are, sir."

The weight of the word pushed Tomkin's shoulders back down. "I'm not a hero."

The enormous man cocked his head, his face earnest. "How do you know?"

Tomkin sighed. *Let me count the ways.* "I've read a lot of stories about heroes."

"Oh." Gerrold looked at Tomkin, then glanced at the tiny lamb in his arms. His brow creased. "Maybe your stories don't talk 'bout all the kinds of heroes there are."

Tomkin looked at the fluff of wooly whiteness engulfed in Gerrold's arms. If only heroics were as easy as giving away one of many lambs to a simple shepherd.

Gerrold turned toward the door. "I'll tell everyone! We'll have a parade when you return!"

A parade? After Tomkin had gone to scavenge eagle feathers?

"Wait!" Tomkin called after the man. Gerrold turned back, puzzled. "I don't think we should tell anyone what is happening. Don't want to...spread panic...."

Gerrold pondered this for a moment, then nodded sagely. "Very clever, sir. May I walk you to the river?"

Tomkin couldn't think of a good reason why not, so he nodded. But he couldn't just carry Scalebreaker out of the hall. He almost put it back, almost explained the truth to Gerrold, but the man was watching him with such admiration, such hope, Tomkin couldn't bring himself to do it.

In the far corner, fastened around Granduncle Horace's armor, was Scalebreaker's scabbard. Tomkin took it and buckled it around his own waist, trying not to imagine how he was going to explain this to his mother.

He walked out of the hall, his hand set casually over the glittering garnet. He and Gerrold walked past the page and out into the cobbled streets of the holding. The afternoon was warm and the people they passed were busy at their shops and trades. Tomkin tried to look nondescript as they passed through the outer wall and the village outside it. As though he were just an average soldier with a sword, instead of the duke's son carrying Scalebreaker. The giant man beside him, shout-whispering encouragements, made it more difficult.

Still, no one took much notice of them. At the docks, Tomkin tucked the sword into the bottom of a small rowboat and headed downriver toward the ruins of Colbreth Castle. Gerrold waved wildly and hurrahed after him until he was around the first bend.

A wave nudged the boat and Scalebreaker clunked against the floor.

"Don't get too excited." he told the sword. "You get a day tucked in the bottom of a rowboat, then it's back on the wall."

The garnet glinted at Tomkin like a tongue of flame, and he sighed.

"I know." He put his back into the next row and the boat slid downstream. "I wish it was really a dragon too."

CHAPTER THREE

Tomkin paddled his small rowboat down the Great River. Alone on the quiet water, Gerrold's story nagged at him. The man was slow, certainly, but would he really mistake a copper eagle for a dragon?

The white rocks along the western bank were stacked in rough layers, creating all sorts of nooks and shelves for bushes and vines to cling to. The farther south Tomkin went, the higher the rocks grew, until he was paddling along the base of a tall, white cliff.

The river carried our hero slowly, steadily toward the castle, through an unusually silent morning. That was bad. No hero had ever passed through an unnaturally silent place and then popped out the other side into normality.

Tomkin paused rowing. The fresh, leafy smell of the river reeds glided past. He could hear birds chirping, but didn't they sound a little too far away? He held his breath, listening.

A shrill squawk from the riverbank gave him such a shock he almost dropped an oar. A brown bird in a bush watched him pass. Tomkin splashed a spray of water at it.

"Fine," he said to the bird, "it's an ordinary day with ordinary noises. But that is very boring."

With a few more strokes, the boat passed around a long, lazy bend. There, sitting halfway up the cliff face, sat the ruins of Castle Colbreth.

Tomkin's breath caught. The ruins were even more perfect than he remembered.

Made from the same white stone as the cliff, it looked as though rocks had pushed out of the ground, stacking themselves into a small walled castle. It had two towers: one round and mostly intact, the other square and squat and falling apart.

The towers were separated by enough space for a small courtyard. The outer wall was dotted with arrow-slit windows, except along the front where three arched windows, huge and empty, gazed out over the river. A thin waterfall cascaded over the cliff above the castle, landed somewhere behind it, and reappeared from a small opening in the front before it plunged the rest of the way to the river.

Tomkin fixed his eyes on the castle, watching for any movement. No wonder Gerrold had thought he'd seen a dragon here. It was the perfect place for one. Now he was here, he almost expected to see a flash of motion in one of the windows.

Bright as death. The phrase wouldn't stop tumbling around in Tomkin's head, feeling less and less like a quirky phrase, and more and more like a warning. This day wasn't going to end with him being eaten by a dragon, was it?

His eyes, caught by the waterfall, followed a patch of the water as it fell, smooth and inevitable, until it crashed onto a jumble of boulders next to the river, shooting spray out in a fine mist.

Past it, the rickety remains of a dock poked out into the river. A handful of weathered posts, fighting to stay upright in the current, showed it had originally reached farther out. But the stub of dock still standing was just large enough to fit Tomkin's little rowboat. He tied his boat as close to the shore as he could, hoping the wood wouldn't rot away before he came back.

He stood and looked at the ruins again. He hadn't planned on taking Scalebreaker to explore with him, but this was starting to feel a bit more like an adventure. And things never went well for adventurers who didn't have their swords. He buckled the scabbard back around his waist and stepped onto the ancient dock. In front of him a jagged, broken line of steps clung to the cliff, zigging and zagging, and occasionally disappearing altogether, up to the castle.

With another tug at the awkward sword, Tomkin began to climb. The first step shifted under his foot, but held. The third tilted under his weight. The twelfth split in half and Tomkin's foot slid off the side. He crashed to his knee and his scabbard whacked him on the back of his leg. His hands scrambled for purchase as the broken piece of step tumbled into the river.

Never mind, he wasn't going to be eaten by a dragon. He was going to die falling down stairs. Typical. His father or brother would at least have made it to the castle to investigate. He took a deep, bracing breath and scrambled higher.

It took ages to reach the top. Tomkin sank to his bruised knees, exhausted, on a small landing facing the main gate of the castle. The view was enough to steal away the little breath he had left. To his right, far below him, was the river. Past it, hills and shaded valleys mingled with each other to the eastern horizon.

To his left, he could see a small lake between the castle and the cliff that continued to rise above it. The waterfall crashed down into it, raising a small cloud of mist.

The thick, wooden castle gate sat before him. Tomkin rose and shoved against it as hard as he could. It didn't move. He yanked and pushed and shook it, but the gate ignored him. He stepped back to consider his options.

The wall of the castle was too smooth to scale. The lake to his left came right up to the castle wall, and he didn't feel like getting wet, so he turned to his right. The ground next to the gate fell away, down at least one story, to the little outcropping of rock the castle wall was built on. It would have been too far down for Tomkin to reach, but a watchtower had crumbled at the corner of the castle, piling enough stones against the wall that it was just a quick scramble for Tomkin to climb down to them. He worked his way along the stones until he reached the front corner of the castle wall.

The rubble from the watchtower continued along the front of the castle, all the way to the first large window looking out over the river. The castle wall sat close to the edge of the cliff along this side, and Tomkin pressed his back to the wall, shuffling along the top of the rubble, refusing to look down. A gust of wind nudged him and he squeezed his eyes shut.

Tomkin's father wouldn't be here, clinging to the wall, creeping along with shaking hands. He would have mounted a full frontal attack on the castle door, breaking it open. Probably with just his fist.

A rock under Tomkin's foot shifted. His eyes flew open and he drew back. The rock rolled down the pile of rubble, bounced into the air, and sailed down, down, down until it was lost in the river. Tomkin's heart felt like it was trying to jump out of his chest and do the same.

He glanced back the way he had come. Maybe he could just turn around and go home.

No.

He wasn't going to leave before he even got inside. Tomkin gritted his teeth and scooted closer, until the base of the first window came within reach. He grabbed the edge and pulled himself onto his stomach on the windowsill. The sill was wide enough to stand on and he climbed to his feet, scooting toward the interior side and away from the sheer drop off behind him.

The room ahead of him was dark compared to the bright sunlight outside, but he could see that the sill he stood on continued along the wall in both directions as a ledge, just wide enough to fit him. The dim impression of the floor was far enough below him that he wasn't interested in jumping. He shuffled along the ledge to his left, away from the window, and waited for his eyes to adjust.

His nose adjusted first. The room smelled dry and metallic —like the armory on a hot day. A moment later Tomkin could make out dark shapes on the walls that might be tattered tapestries. The floor of the room was dotted with lumps— broken furniture, perhaps.

Below him, mounded against the wall beneath the ledge, was an enormous pile of...something. Tomkin leaned forward and caught a glimpse of bright orange.

His first thought was a pile of garnets, like the one in his sword, and his breath caught at the thought of so much wealth.

But at that moment a cloud passed out from in front of the sun, the room brightened, and the entire mound turned into a pile of orange...

Scales.

Tomkin was perched on a ledge above a fire-orange dragon.

CHAPTER FOUR

TOMKIN DREW IN A SHARP BREATH, then clamped his lips shut against the noise of it.

Slowly, he drew his sword.

He could make out the shape of the dragon now, its back curled along the wall, its head and tail wrapped in front of its enormous body.

Tomkin's legs began to shake and he pressed back against the wall. He shifted his weight back toward the window, holding his breath until he could step back outside and flee.

No. He clamped down on his fear.

Elton wouldn't run away. He'd stride in, blond hair flowing, charming smile flashing, and kill the beast in one, swift, muscly stroke.

There was no way Tomkin could do that. His hair never flowed that nicely, for one thing. But he was standing over a dragon—a real dragon—and he couldn't be a coward now. He couldn't fight it, but there must be something useful he could learn before he left. Some weakness he could find, a missing scale perhaps...

Placing each foot carefully, determined to ignore his shaking legs, he took several steps further along the wall.

Below him, the rounded heap of blazing orange scales rose and fell.

Bright as death.

Tomkin clenched his jaw and shoved the phrase out of his mind.

He set the tip of the heavy sword on the ledge next to him. The orange garnet in the hilt glinted, an orange almost as bright as the dragon's scales. Tomkin ran his gaze over the dragon's side. The creature was covered with smooth scales except for a line of jagged spines along the ridge of its back, snaking down to the tip of its tail. Leathery orange wings were folded tight along the spines.

But there were no weaknesses. Nothing but an unbroken wall of scales. Tomkin searched again. There had to be a missing scale. There was always a chink in the armor. How else did anyone defeat dragons?

This one, however, appeared chinkless. Scale after perfect scale covered the creature. The color was mesmerizing...like the brightest orange part of a flame. Tomkin leaned forward to see further around the monster's belly. As the dragon breathed, the light rippled across it in waves of burnished bronze and blinding yellow.

Maybe on the dragon's neck he'd find a weakness? He crept forward. His hand felt slick on the hilt of the sword.

There, on its neck was...something. A dark spot? A missing scale? Tomkin peered down, trying to catch the light moving across the creature's neck. There was *something*.

He grabbed a wooden beam running up the wall next to him and leaned out.

What was that smudge of darkness? He leaned out further.

It was...

...a leaf. Just a leaf.

With a loud crack the beam sagged forward. Tomkin

clutched it, the splintery edge of the wood cutting into his hand.

Below him the dragon shifted and raised its head. Two folds of scales parted, revealing a reptilian eye, yellow and savage.

Tomkin's heart faltered. The eye stared straight at him. Straight through him.

His body felt...wrong. His skin too tingly, his heart too big and fast. His lungs wouldn't breathe right.

The dragon's head turned like a snake's, pinning Tomkin with an unblinking stare.

The wood beam cracked again, and Tomkin grabbed at it with both hands—realizing too late that meant he'd let go of the sword. His heart stopped altogether, his eyes locked on the silver blade as it glinted and fell towards the dragon's side, growing smaller and more insignificant.

The dragon's eyes followed the blade as well. It didn't shift or cringe. For the briefest moment Tomkin imagined the blade piercing the dragon's scales, driving deep into its body, delivering a death blow. But the sword twisted, the heavy hilt tumbling below the blade. When it hit, it was the garnet at the end of the hilt that tinked harmlessly off the scales. The blade clattered down the dragon's side and there was a flash of orange as the garnet broke out of the hilt and skittered away past the dragon's tail. A low growl emanated from the its chest.

Tomkin stood rooted to the ledge, his eyes staring at the dark floor where the garnet had landed.

His father was going to kill him.

That thought was so stupid that a short huff of laughter burst out of him. It echoed off the walls, sounding unhinged. Tomkin felt the dragon's gaze rise from the blade until it skewered him to the wall. The rest of its body lay relaxed.

It's going to eat me. Tomkin imagined the mouth opening,

the dragon's head striking forward impossibly fast. The teeth sinking into his body.

But the dragon didn't move. It didn't even twitch the end of its tail. Didn't dragons always twitch their tails? Maybe that was cats.

Tomkin's mind felt frantic, jumping from one thought to the next.

He felt the pressure of the dragon's gaze like a heat pressing against him. It was like standing close to the baker's oven where the air pushed against his skin. The bread weathering that heat suddenly seemed brave.

That was the moment when Tomkin realized he was not brave. Others were made to be the bread, to survive the fire and not burn up. Tomkin was made to stay in the library reading and waiting for someone to fix him a sandwich.

No, that metaphor was just weird. It would leave Tomkin eating the hero.

Tomkin dragged his mind back to the moment and blinked. The dragon did not.

The silence and stillness stretched on, building its own sort of menace. Tomkin's heart had swelled to fill his entire body. He could feel it pounding in his ears, in his fingers, his entire chest thrummed with it. His throat was so full of his heart it didn't have room to take in any air.

The silence grew so terrible that it was worse than the scales, worse than the slitted, unmoving pupils. Everything inside of Tomkin changed from wanting to run to wanting to break the silence.

It rose like a wave inside him, an irrepressible urge. Tomkin pressed his lips together, but it was no good. He'd never been able to keep his mouth shut. The pressure built and built until it squeaked out of him. Like a mouse being strangled.

"Hellocchh." Tomkin clamped his lips shut. That had not been a manly noise.

The dragon's head cocked.

Tomkin cleared his throat and tried again. "Hello."

The dragon did not move, but Tomkin couldn't stay frozen any longer. The stillness was as bad as the silence. Tomkin pulled one hand off the wood and gave a little wave.

Under his other hand, the beam shifted, then tore off the wall. Tomkin scrambled, reaching for anything. His fingers scraped over the rocky wall, scattering dust and pebbles. There was nothing to grab.

Tomkin fell.

He plummeted toward the dragon and a scream ripped out of him. He imagined crashing into the dragon a hundred times before he finally slammed into it. He tumbled and rolled over the scales, just like his impotent sword, before crumpling onto the stone floor.

Pain shot through his shoulder and one of his knees throbbed. He clenched his mouth shut to keep from screaming again. If he was going to die, he wasn't going to do it squealing like a helpless victim. Even if that was precisely what he was.

He shoved himself over onto his back.

The dragon lifted one clawed hand high in the air above him. Tomkin's mind shut out everything else. The palm was covered with small, perfect scales. Pale orange, like a faded flower. Four long claws, each longer than Tomkin's forearm, narrowed into black spikes.

Smooth and silent, the dragon lowered it, stopping just above Tomkin. Two claws clicked on the stones to Tomkin's left. One scraped along the floor to his right. The last claw pressed against his chest.

Tomkin could feel his heart pounding against the tip of it. The dragon brought its head close to him and drew in a deep breath. Light rippled across its scales. Tomkin's gaze was drawn along with it. The creature was enormous. Tomkin's entire body was smaller than the beast's arm.

The dragon breathed out, and Tomkin shrank away, waiting for the flames. All that came was a wave of hot air, smelling like beloved things being burned to char.

You dare disturb me? The dragon's voice reverberated inside Tomkin's skull, deep and threatening, like a drum deep in the earth.

Tomkin flinched, horrified. The dragon was speaking directly into his mind. He tried to swallow, but there was something wrong with his throat.

The dragon's eyes narrowed. *Who are you?*

"T-t-tomkin Th-th-thornhewn."

The dragon looked at the sword, then back at Tomkin, his gaze inexorable and accusing.

"Sorry about the sword," Tomkin said. "I didn't mean to...." His voice trailed off. He had been poised over the dragon with a drawn sword. That was a difficult thing to explain away. "I thought you were an eagle," he said in a small voice.

The dragon let out a low growl and its palm dropped a handbreadth, pressing Tomkin against the floor.

"I mean...I didn't...I...." His heart was pounding against the pressure of the claw. "You had a leaf on your neck," he finished lamely.

The dragon's voice rolled into his mind again, quiet and lethal. *I do not wish to be disturbed.*

"That makes sense," Tomkin said quickly, nodding. "You picked a remote location for your lair. I didn't mean to bother you. I can just go...."

The dragon cocked its head. It looked at Tomkin for another eternity with that fathomless gaze. Then it drew back its claws and its open jaws darted forward.

Tomkin screamed again.

The dragon's teeth snapped shut. Smooth, hard teeth scraped against Tomkin's stomach and he was lifted off the floor by his shirt.

He grabbed for purchase and found himself clinging to a large, white fang. The teeth pulled his shirt tight around him and the point of one long fang pressed against Tomkin's ribs. He shoved himself against the dragon's teeth and lips, trying to rip his shirt free, but none of the fabric gave.

Tomkin's breath rushed in and out, but he still wasn't getting enough air. He pounded his fists against the dragon's snout, but to no effect. The dragon moved deeper into the hall, its scales rasping along the stone floor. Tomkin kept expecting the jaws to open and snap shut around him, but the dragon just carried him. They climbed a wide stairway at the far end of the room, out into the sunlight. Tomkin blinked at the brightness and twisted around looking for help.

He was being carried through a courtyard between the castle's two towers. Sunlight bounced off the white stones as though this were just a normal summer afternoon, not the last moments of Tomkin's life.

The dragon carried him to the circular tower. Tomkin craned his neck to see a barred wooden door at its base. With one long, black claw, the dragon lifted the bar and pulled the door open. Then, with a toss of its head, it flung Tomkin in.

CHAPTER FIVE

TOMKIN CRASHED down onto something lumpy. There was a splintering of wood and a cry of pain he was positive hadn't come from himself.

The door slammed shut and the bar clunked into place, dropping the tower into a deep gloom. A wave of relief at being alive washed over Tomkin until a sharp jab dug into his back.

"Get off me!" The lumpy thing shoved at him.

Tomkin tried to sit up, but the person under him, a girl from the voice, kept shifting and kicking.

A girl! The dragon had captured a girl!

His scabbard caught on something and ripped off. A small foot pressed into his back and shoved, sending him tumbling forward to crash into a pile of rocks. Pain shot across his shoulder and he rolled over, groaning. Sitting among broken pieces of a chair in front of a sagging desk was a furious girl. She was tremendously dirty. Her hair, which might have been brown, was tangled and held small clods of dirt and her face was smudgy with mud. She was like some fantastical creature made of earth.

Tomkin scrambled to his feet and held a hand out to her.

"Don't worry," he whispered, "it'll be okay. I'll get you out of here. Are there any other doors?" He peered through the dim light.

She scrambled up and crossed her arms, looking remarkably imperious for a girl dressed in dirt.

"Get out." Her voice rang in the hollow tower.

Tomkin blinked. "Out?"

"Out." She pointed at the door. "This is mine."

Tomkin looked around, confusion putting a damper on his terror.

"What's yours?" He was standing in the bottom of the round tower, which rose two or three stories. High above him, sunlight poured in through a ring of thin, arched windows, but only a dribble of it reached down to where they were. The skeleton of a staircase clung to the wall in bits and pieces. Thick, rotten beams stuck out overhead from what had been a second floor. The air smelled dusty and old, as though it had been held captive in these walls too. "This tower? I think the dragon's using it as a prison."

She raised her sharp little chin and looked down her sharp little nose at him. "It's not a prison. It's the keep."

Tomkin looked at the pile of rubble on the floor beside them. "No, it's not. Keeps are…strongholds, the last, best refuge of a castle." He let out a little laugh. "This is more of a 'give up' than a 'keep.'"

Her eyes narrowed to venomous slits. "Call it whatever you like. It's *mine*."

She seemed serious.

Tomkin sank onto the pile of rocks behind him, rubbing his sore shoulder. His terror had drained away, leaving his muscles feeling weak and watery. "We've been captured by a *dragon*. Nothing about this place is ours."

"I haven't been captured. I'm here by choice."

Tomkin stared at her. "By choice? Inside that barred door?"

She glared at him. "Who are you? Some little squire who thought it would be impressive to kill a dragon?"

He drew himself up. "I'm the son of the Duke of Marshwell." He paused to let the significance of that sink in.

The girl's eyebrow twitched the slightest amount and she appraised him again. Tomkin pulled his shoulders back. Common girls were so easily impressed.

She raised one eyebrow in disdain. "*You're* the future Duke of Marshwell?"

That settled it. Tomkin didn't like her. "No, I'm the duke's younger son. My brother Elton will be duke."

"What will you be?"

"I'll be me," he snapped. "Tomkin of Marshwell, with the full force of Marshwell's troops and powers supporting me. I'll be anything I want to be."

She gave him a little smirk. "Except duke."

Tomkin hated her. "Who are you and why are you here?"

She tossed her hair, sending up a little puff of dust. "Vorath and I have an agreement."

"Vorath?"

"The dragon. You didn't even introduce yourself to him, did you? I didn't realize younger sons of lesser lords had so few manners."

Lesser lords! He spoke slowly so he could get through to her. "You know what Marshwell is, right? It's this land you live on. Stretching north to the Blue Hills and south to Coastal Baylon. It's the third largest duchy in the kingdom. And," he said, remembering the Isle of Bald Sheep, "we even have an island."

The girl looked unimpressed. "Don't forget the putrid marshes."

"They're not putrid, they're…mournful."

She snorted. "It'd make me mournful if my land was covered with them."

"It's not covered—the marshes are one small part."

"Then why's it called Marshwell?"

Tomkin took a deep breath. He didn't just hate this girl. What was a word worse than hate? Nothing came to mind. He'd just capitalize it then. He Hated this girl. "So, you're friends with the dragon?"

"Of course. I talked to him when I met him this morning. What did you do? Run at him with a sword?"

"No." Whatever he had done, it hadn't involved running. "What did you talk about?"

"I pointed out to Vorath that it's late summer and the cattle drives are next week. I could gather a dozen cattle for him with an hour or two of work. He'd have food for weeks."

Tomkin stared at her, stunned. "You're domesticating him?"

The girl snorted. "No one domesticates a dragon. We're working together." She lifted her chin again. "It's a mutually beneficial association."

She was either insane, or incredibly stupid. "Right. Vorath gets cows. How do you benefit? Besides not being eaten until the cows run out?"

"He's not going to eat me. I get to live here. I pointed out to Vorath that his castle wasn't in great shape and I could help with that if, in return, he would let me live here with him. I could give him a castle worth being proud of and he could give me a home." She straightened her shoulders. "I'm not interested in living the life people think I should live. I'm writing my own story."

Writing her own story? Someone needed to take away this girl's quill. "Wait, did you come *looking* for a dragon?"

"No." She stared at him like he was an idiot. Like *he* was the idiot! "I was looking for a new home. Serendipitously, I met Vorath."

Serendipitously was a big word for such a dusty girl.

"And now that I'm here, well...." She stood as tall as a

small girl could. "This is my new home. It has a lot of potential."

"It has the potential to fall into the river."

Her eyebrows drew down sharply like a pair of angry dirt clods. "Tell me this, Tomkin the Inept Dragon Hunter, why didn't the Duke of Marshwell send a warrior to fight Vorath?"

Tomkin shifted. "It was my decision. I'm in charge of Marshwell while my father is fighting at the border." Tomkin raised his own chin.

She studied him. "They left you in charge?"

Tomkin gave her his most imperious nod. It didn't feel as polished as hers.

"And instead of coming up with a good plan, you came yourself?"

"I'm perfectly capable—," he began.

"Obviously."

"—and once I do this, my father will drop his foolish ideas about who he wants me to marry and things can get back to normal."

She stared at him, appalled. "You…you came to fight a dragon because you didn't want to get married?"

"No. Marriage is fine. I'd like to get married. I just don't want to marry the girl my father picked."

"Why not? Is she not rich enough for the littlest son of the Duke of the Putrid Marshes?"

"It has nothing to do with that! The rumors about her are enough to—"

"Rumors?" she interrupted. "Based on only rumors you're willing to fight a dragon to get away from her?"

"It's not just about her. If the younger son of a…less prominent lord is going to attract the eye of someone…significant, he's got to have some sort of claim. Something impressive."

"Like being captured by a dragon?"

He tried to glare the smirk off her face. If his brother had tried this ill-conceived plan, he would have found some beautiful, rich maiden trapped here. And she'd be nice. He'd have found his soulmate, who also happened to be the exact ally his father would need to cement the peace between Queensland and Coastal Baylon.

And Tomkin had found this girl. Mean, selfish, and crazy.

"Look, we have to get out of here, and I need to kill the dragon."

"You're not killing Vorath," she said matter-of-factly.

"Yes, I am. Mostly to save my land, but also, as much as you don't see it, to save you. He's a dragon. He may enjoy your cattle for a bit, but then he's going to eat you."

"I suppose that all depends on how good of friends we are by then," she said primly. "I wouldn't expect you to understand. You're one of those people who judge everyone the instant you meet them and never give them a chance."

Tomkin clamped down on the rage growing in his chest. "Fine. Stay here. Get eaten. But while I'm stuck with you, do me a favor and shut your mouth."

He stomped over to the door and yanked on it. It didn't budge. The hinges were solid, the wood strong. It figured the only part of this place that wasn't rotten was this door.

Behind him, he heard the girl shoving things around. A twinge of guilt threaded its way through his boiling mass of anger. The "shut your mouth" bit had been harsh. She was just a girl. She was probably scared.

He took a deep breath and turned to face her, forcing his voice to sound polite. "I'm sorry." The words sounded almost genuine. "What's your name?"

She pointed at her shut mouth.

And the rage was back. "I said I was sorry!"

She rolled her eyes.

"Fine. I'll pick a name for you. What's a good one for a smudgy, shabby-looking girl who's mean and bossy?"

Tomkin took a grim pleasure in the glare she flashed at him.

"I suppose it's obvious. In any good story, you'd be a shrew. Magwina the Shrew."

Her eyes narrowed.

"Mind if I call you Mags for short?"

She gave a huff and turned back around to her broken chair.

"Now, Mags, I need to find a way out of here before the dragon eats me."

"He's not going to eat you," Mags said, exasperated. "Or he would have done it already."

Tomkin paused. That was a good point. "Why *didn't* he eat me?"

She rolled her eyes. "Because he's not the bloodthirsty monster you think he is."

Tomkin shook his head. "That's not it." Only a crazy person like Mags would believe that. "He must want something. What does he want?"

"To not be attacked with a sword?"

"Trust me, swords aren't much of a threat to him."

Why had the dragon thrown him in here with Mags? He looked at the girl, who was stacking her wood pieces with a scowl.

A dragon who didn't eat people and a girl who collected pieces of shattered furniture. This story was so bizarre Tomkin didn't even know where to begin fixing it.

She continued to shove debris around.

"What are you looking for?" he demanded. "A splinter?"

"I'm looking for a missing nail."

"Why? You can't fix that chair. It's broken."

"Ahh," she said, not turning towards him, "I forgot I should run all my ideas past you. Your own plans seem to work out so well." She picked up the nail and dropped it on the desk. "There's the last one."

"Right," Tomkin muttered, "you play with your wood chips. I'm going to figure out a way out of here."

CHAPTER SIX

TOMKIN WALKED over to the door and peered through a large crack. "I can see a sliver of the courtyard," he reported. "It looks deserted."

"This is a castle," Mags said. "You don't call it a courtyard, it's the bailey."

Tomkin rolled his eyes. "The *bailey* looks deserted."

He tried to see the bar holding the door closed. Maybe he could squeeze something through the crack to lift it. He tried to shove a small piece of wood through, but it didn't work. "This door isn't going to budge."

"Shocking." Mags began matching broken chair pieces to each other.

Tomkin looked around. Above the door, along the curved wall of the tower, a crescent of the second floor still clung to some rotting wooden beams. What remained of the staircase reached up to it. More or less.

He moved to the bottom of the stairs and set a foot on the first step. The wood creaked, but held.

The stairs complained at his weight, but he reached the highest step safely. Unfortunately, the last four steps were missing, leaving a wide gap between himself and the second floor. It was within reach, if he lunged, but the edge of the floor was just broken planks, clinging to their neighbors by a few tenacious fibers. A rug, molded and moth-eaten, ran all the way to the wall, where it was pinned by a pile of rocks. If he could reach it, he could use it to pull himself up. Tomkin gauged the jump, and leapt.

Below him Mags gasped.

He slammed into the floor and the sharp edge of the wood jabbed into his stomach. He grabbed the rug. The piece of wood beneath him cracked. His body lurched lower, his legs swung wildly.

"Don't fall!" called Mags.

"You're not helping!" He pulled on the wad of rug and tried to throw one of his legs onto the floor. There was a long, low ripping sound and the rug began to slide.

"What's ripping?" demanded Mags. "Are you destroying my castle?"

"Shut"—Tomkin grabbed for something else, anything else— "up!" His fingers jabbed into a sharp hole in a plank, sending shooting pain into his hand but stopping his slide. With a great effort and a lot of pain, Tomkin got one leg up, then the other, then rolled onto his back, gasping for breath. Below him the wood made a fracturing noise.

"Do *not* knock that entire floor down," Mags said.

He wanted to wiggle and see what fell on her. Instead, he rolled to his side and onto his feet. The floor beneath him shifted. Thinking light thoughts about clouds and butterflies, Tomkin stepped over to the wall where it was more stable.

He set his back against the wall and looked up. The windows were still high above him, almost twice as high as he could reach.

Tomkin ran his hands along the rough stone wall. Maybe he could climb. He put his fingertips into a crack and squashed his foot into a nook. He had never climbed a rock wall before, but it couldn't be that hard. It was just like climbing a ladder, right? He managed to lift himself knee-high before his fingers and forearms began to burn.

"What are you doing up there?"

Mags' voice startled him and his foot slipped, crashing down. There was a deep, resonant crack from beneath him and he froze, clinging to the wall. The floor shifted to the right.

"Do *not* break my keep!"

Tomkin didn't move. "All of your yelling is not helping," he said through his teeth.

"I am more than willing to help, if you would bother to ask. But since you like to throw yourself into action without putting the slightest thought into whether or not it's a good idea...."

"Then come up here and help me reach this window so I can get a view outside." That girl was the most horrible person he had ever met. He was almost tempted to leave her here when he escaped. He could just slip through the window, climb down the outside of the tower—after he got the hang of this rock climbing thing—and slip away. She could stay in her broken tower cooing at her dragon until he ate her.

Mags began to mutter something below him. Tomkin stretched his hand a little higher up the wall, dragging his fingers along the small gaps between the stones. He needed smaller fingers. How did people do this? The rest of the wall was the same, with the exception of one knob of rock just out of reach that stuck out a handbreadth. If he could reach that and somehow scramble on top of it, he could reach the window. He stretched as far as he could, his fingers brushing the underside of it.

Beneath him, Mags was still talking.

Another voice answered her. It was low, but gruff.

"Who's down there?" Tomkin demanded.

"Don't interrupt," Mags snipped. Then, addressing the

other person, she said, "See? He claimed to be the Duke of Marshwell's son, but he has the manners of a farm boy."

"Who are you talking to?" Tomkin craned his neck around, but could only see the broken crescent of floor below him and the skeletal husk of stairs spiraling down the far wall.

He received no answer, so he swung his hand toward the rock again. This time, when he missed, his foot slipped out of the crack it was in and he slid, landing hard on his heel and crashing onto his back. He braced for the brittle floor to collapse, hardly daring to breathe.

It stayed firm. He shifted his weight. Nothing happened. It felt strong and…floor-like. He stood and gave a little jump. A hollow drum sound reverberated through the tower, but nothing shifted, cracked, or even wiggled.

"Will you stop?" Mags' voice floated up, annoyed.

At the edge of the floor, something moved. Two thin sticks waved around for a moment, then leaned on the edge of the planks.

"Oh, thank you, it's perfect!" Mags said, her voice surprisingly kind. "You do such fine work. Would you mind holding the bottom while I climb?"

Tomkin took a step toward the edge. "Is that a ladder?"

The sticks wiggled for a couple moments, then Mags' dirty head popped into view.

"Be careful!" Tomkin reached one hand out towards her.

"Don't tell me what to do." Mags threw an annoyed glare at him. She climbed onto the floor.

Tomkin tried to stifle his annoyance. "That wood is rotten."

She rolled her eyes at him, then turned to look down the ladder. "This whole center section is strong?"

"Yes, mistress. It's perfectly safe." Another head popped over the edge. This one was not nearly as dirty as Mags, and not nearly as human.

CHAPTER SEVEN

THE CREATURE HOPPING over the top of the ladder was a bit like a child. The top of its head was only a bit above Mags' waist. But it had a mustache of two stringy tails of hair and large, knobby fingers that reminded Tomkin of tree roots. Its enormous features were drawn into a scowl that looked remarkably like Mags.

"What is that thing?" Tomkin said, leaning forward to get a better look. It wore little purple clothes and a purple cap above its enormous pointed ears.

Mags flashed Tomkin a look of venom. "This is Wink." She set her hand on the creature's head. "He is a kobold and my friend."

A kobold! Tomkin stared at the creature. He had never seen one of the magical little creatures, reputed to be able to fix any broken thing. Tomkin had expected a kobold to look more pleasant, more benevolent. This one did not, but maybe that was because he was glowering at Tomkin.

"Yes," the kobold said, addressing Mags in a gravelly voice, "the center of the floor is safe. You can cross to where the boy is. If he bothers you, just shove him off to either side. Those parts won't hold an oaf like him."

"Thank you," Mags said, leaning down and kissing the top of the little cap. She looked around. "Wink, can you do anything with this rug? I think I need a new dress."

The kobold ran his hand along the rug, drawing out tangles of thread. He held them toward the window, tugging on them. Giving an approving nod, he pulled a little knife out of his belt and sliced off a small section. The moldy cloth disappeared beneath his jacket.

Mags walked across the floor toward Tomkin.

Tomkin tapped his foot experimentally. It felt solid. "How did you do that?" he asked Wink. "Did you prop it up on something?"

The kobold gave him a withering look and turned back to Mags. "Is there anything else you need?"

"Nothing else. Thank you, Wink."

"Then please be careful, mistress."

Mags smiled fondly at the creature before crossing over to stand next to Tomkin. Wink, with a final glare at him, disappeared, and Tomkin was left staring at an empty patch of floor.

"That's amazing! He really fixed the wood. I've never met a kobold before. Did you catch it? Or did you have to rescue it? Yes, that's how you get one, right? You rescue it?"

Mags scowled at him. "I didn't rescue him. Wink has lived with our family for years. A kobold will take up residence with you if you are kind to it."

Tomkin looked over to where she'd come up. "A ladder!" He ran to the edge to see it. The rungs were smooth and even, the edges sanded to a polish. Tomkin ran his hand along the top rung. This was his way up to the window. Except it was too long, probably almost twice as long as the distance from where he stood to the window.

"We'll have to break it." Tomkin began to pull the ladder up.

"We will not!" Mags declared. "Put that down!"

Tomkin turned back to her. "Why? We need to get out of here."

Mags' eyes narrowed and she considered Tomkin for a long moment. When she spoke, her voice was overly kind, as though she were explaining something to a dim child. "Do you understand we're not in danger? I don't want to leave this tower. I don't want to leave this castle. This is my home. And Wink is going to help me fix it until it is the nicest castle anyone has ever seen.

"You," she gave him a pitying smile, "obviously, can't live here, because even though you seem well-meaning, you're clearly unbalanced. So I will help you look out the window to see what's going on, and then you're on your own." Her brow crinkled. "I feel obliged to tell you, I think you're making a big mistake trying to run and I don't see it ending well."

He was unbalanced? Tomkin bit back the words that jumped to mind. He needed her help, so he curled his lips into what he hoped was a smile. "Thanks for the warning. Let's just get this over with. If I lift you up, can you get onto that little rock sticking out? From there you should be able to see out the window."

Mags looked at the rock, unenthused.

"Wait!" Tomkin said, turning back to where he'd last seen Wink. How hadn't he thought of this sooner? "Wink! Make us another ladder! That would be easier, right? Then I'll climb up myself and I don't have to bother you at all. Wink! Pop into view again. I need a ladder. Ooh! And a rope long enough to reach the ground from the window." He looked around the room for the creature. "And something to anchor it, just something that will keep it in the window." He glanced at Mags. "Then you could claim to not know how I got out…."

She was glaring at him. "Wink is not going to make anything for you. It's not easy for him to make these things. It takes a lot out of him."

"Okay, fine," Tomkin said, clenching his fists. "Then can you please try to look out the window?"

Mags wrinkled her nose, but nodded. Tomkin leaned against the wall, and Mags, with a lot of scrambling and two good knees to his head, climbed up until her feet were planted on Tomkin's shoulders and his face was against the bottom of her heavy skirt. It was partly awkward, partly suffocating. Dust and dirt swirled around his head, choking him. He turned his head to the side, gasping for breath.

"How on earth did you get this dirty?" He coughed.

"You'd be dirty too if you had to cross the dirt flats during a wind storm. Stop wiggling so I can get on this rock."

The dirt flats? She'd come from that far east? Mags' shoes dug into his shoulders and the dust stung his eyes. With a sharp jab of her boot, Mags shoved herself onto the little outcropping of rock.

"I can see out!" she hollered, leaning her head out the window.

"Shhh!" Tomkin hissed, moving away from the wall and her dirt.

She waved one hand at him dismissively. The window was neck high and she was peering out, surrounded by a cloud of dust, sparkling and swirling in the sunbeam. "These walls are thick, which is great for my keep, but I can't see out too well. They're so thick I could lie across the sill here. Hang on...." She put both her arms out and heaved herself up until he could only see her thick, dark skirt and the soles of her boots.

"What do you see?"

"Well, there's a lovely sunset." Mags' voice came back muffled from outside the window.

"I don't care about the sunset! Can you see the dragon?"

"No. Everything looks deserted."

Tomkin waited for her to continue, but she gave no more information. He could hear her humming and her feet swung jauntily. "I'm so very glad you're enjoying yourself, and I hate to interrupt, but, can you see anything about the castle? Is there a way to get down from where you are? Any obvious escape routes? Anything *useful* you can tell me?"

"Well," her voice came back smugly, "my keep has sheer walls, as it should. I don't want enemies to be able to scale the walls up to these windows. Wink will be so pleased. He just has the interior to work on, and he's so wonderful at interior work, it will be done in no time. If you climbed out of here, you would fall to your death."

Of course it was sheer. This day wasn't going to make anything easy for him. If Elton had been trapped in here, there would have been a strategic crumbling section of the wall providing a dangerous, but ultimately heroic, way to escape. "Well, what else do you see? Is the castle wall intact? Are there any exits besides the main gate? Is there a route up the cliffs?"

Mags didn't answer.

"What are you doing up there?"

"Sorry, I didn't realize it was so late. It's rather dark in the bailey. I suppose that's because we're snuggled up to these cliffs on the west. It's all shadowy and dramatic in the courtyard. I'm so pleased I found this place. This will be the finest castle in Queensland.

"But the truly stunning thing is that there are enormous storm clouds brewing to the east and they're the most beautiful shades of red and orange. They're very similar to Vorath's colors, don't you think? Oh, you can't see them, but you can imagine. They are just like Vorath's scales. I do think he's the prettiest dragon I've ever seen."

"Because you've seen so many dragons?" Tomkin said, annoyed.

"I've seen plenty of paintings of dragons," her voice came back primly. "I think orange might be an unusual color. There are loads of red and black dragons, but Vorath is such a fiery orange, like the brightest bit of flame at the bottom of a candle."

Tomkin scowled. That had been his exact thoughts when he'd seen the scales.

"Oh! The clouds *are* exactly the right color! Vorath is right there, flying out of them and I can barely tell him apart from the clouds!"

"Get back!" Tomkin hissed.

"Hello!" Mags called, her body thrashing about enough that Tomkin could imagine her waving enthusiastically.

"Knock it off!" he whispered loudly. "We're not *supposed* to be escaping!"

"It's Vorath," Mags called, as though he hadn't heard. "He's coming back from across the river and he has…something in his claws. A sheep maybe? Now why didn't he ask me for help? I would have gotten one for him."

She was going to get herself killed! She was going to get them both killed!

"Hello!" she called out the window. After a short pause she continued, "Yes, that would be nice. But how will I—Oooh!"

Tomkin lunged for her feet, but they were too high. With a slither, Mags' legs shot up and disappeared through the window.

Tomkin caught a flash of orange scales before the blue sky out the window was left perfectly empty.

PART II

The hero was supposed to slay the dragon and rescue the maiden,
Tomkin was sure of it.

But if that were true,
then Tomkin was left with the unpleasant realization
that there was no hero around.

-From Keeper Gerone's retelling
of Tomkin and the Dragon

CHAPTER EIGHT

TOMKIN STARED at the empty window, his hand stretched up for Mags' absent foot, the breath sucked from his lungs.

He listened for screams or cries, but heard nothing.

"Wink!" he called out, looking around the tower frantically. "Wink! Can you hear me? Mags is in trouble! Wink!"

The tower was still. The sunbeams streaming in the western windows were clouded with the dirt from Mags. Beyond that, nothing moved, nothing stirred. The walls of the tower closed around him, cutting him off from the rest of the world.

Tomkin rushed to the ladder and climbed down. He ran to the door and threw himself against it. Pain shot through his sore shoulder again, but the door didn't budge. He shoved at it, pounded on it, kicked it. The door refused to acknowledge him.

With a groan, Tomkin sank to the floor, leaning back on the door. A distant rumble of thunder rolled across the sky. Mags' thunderstorm. The thunder ended and silence flowed back into the tower, as though Tomkin were the only thing left alive. There was no father coming to help, no brother, no friend. Not even a shrew to argue with. He was utterly alone and utterly trapped.

Thunder growled again, closer this time.

He cocked his head to listen. The thunderstorm might be a blessing. Even a dragon wouldn't hear someone creeping around if there was a thunderstorm going on.

Tomkin pushed himself off the wall. This problem just needed to be attacked step by step. First, find a way out of this tower. Second, find his sword. Third, find Mags. Which was a lot of finding, but Tomkin was better at finding than fighting, so it just might work.

The garnet. His heart dropped a little. The garnet had broken off the hilt. That was a problem for later. First, he needed to get out of this tower. He stood and surveyed the keep again. There was nothing useful. It was a mess.

Mags' cobbled-together desk held an assortment of papers and a bowl of apples. Tomkin's stomach growled and he grabbed one of them before glancing at the top paper, which featured a sketch labelled "Keep Interior - First Floor." Quick lines roughed out a hulking fireplace, one of the arrow-slit windows with floor-length curtains, and a nook deep under the stairs with this little desk, the chair, and a long bookshelf.

The bookshelf idea was a good one. It fit well in the space. That's where Tomkin would sit, if it existed. He'd build a fire in the fireplace, because empty fireplaces looked malevolent, then he'd go over to this nook and find a good book.

Tiny notes labeled the nook.

Need wax for candle, iron and glass for lantern.

Desk fits perfectly. Would love cushion on chair.

Need good ink and better quill.

Shelf will hold only 20-30 books. The last words were written slower than the rest, as though contemplatively. "Only" was underlined twice.

Her handwriting was surprisingly nice. She must be more

educated than he had assumed. And the sketches were decent, too. He couldn't have drawn them.

He went to set the page down, and saw the paper underneath it was a letter written in the same thin, precise writing. There was no mistaking that this was written by someone well educated. There was an elaborate yet pleasing flourish on the "F" at the beginning of the addressee's name.

A long drawing of Colbreth Castle cascaded down the right side of the paper. The upper cliffs rose, tall and solid-looking, and unbroken stairs clung to the lower cliff down to the river. The castle itself was drawn in bolder strokes than the rest of the sketch, standing regally on an outcropping of rock. The round tower, which now deserved the name "keep," rose sternly from the left side of the castle, and the squat square tower flew splendid flags snapping in the wind.

Tomkin looked at the castle for a long time. The drawing was fantastic. The lines of the towers and walls surged up, steadfast and proud. The castle was...well, it was a good castle. A great castle. Once the dragon was gone, maybe Tomkin could convince his father Colbreth Castle should be restored. It would be magnificent.

He didn't mean to begin reading the letter. But the decorated F led him into the word "Father."

Father,

I do hope you are not alarmed at my absence. I assure you I am well. I could not stay another day, though. I cannot be like mother. I cannot run the house as she did. And knowing I was failing every day, knowing I can never replace what we lost when she died, it felt like I was drowning. I have trained Lidia over the past few months. She will be able to keep the house running smoothly. She is the easier daughter.

I am terribly afraid you will blame yourself, but please believe me this is best for both of us. I know your plans for me were good for our family, even good for me, but I can't bear to disappoint you anymore than I already have. I doubt I am really the answer you need.

I know people will talk. I have left rumors with the staff that I am traveling to court for a few months. That should stave off questions for a while. No one from the house should be traveling to court now that winter is coming, so my secret should be safe until I am finished.

I am starting a new home, Father. One that is glorious and small and within my power to run. I think I shall do a good job of it and I do hope, when I have finished setting it right, you will come for a long visit.

I miss you dearly. Tell Lidia I love her and that she will do an excellent job filling mother's shoes. Much better than I would have. I'm so sorry for al—

The letter ended and Tomkin flipped it over, as though it would continue. As though she hadn't been interrupted by Tomkin being flung in the door and landing on top of her.

He set the paper down gently, remembering how smudgy her face was when he had first met her. How hadn't he noticed it had been from tears? When he'd landed on Mags, she'd been crying.

Tomkin read the end of the letter again. He needed to get out of here. He needed to find Mags and convince her to go back home to her father.

He looked around the tower. The door was the only real option, of course, but it was thick and solid and the handle was broken. He could just barely see the bar holding the door closed.

This was another thing Mags could have done that would have been useful. She could have fixed the door handle so she could get out. And so he could get out. What had she been doing in here?

Tomkin searched the room, picking up anything that looked thin and strong enough to move the bar. There wasn't much. Mags' chair had been fixed. Wink must have fixed it while Tomkin was up above. A chair. Out of all the things she *could* have done, she fixed a chair. It wasn't even a very nice chair. Just a plain guard's chair.

What he should do is smash it again and use the pieces to try to get out. But he left it and found a couple thin slivers of wood. They broke as soon as he tried to lift the heavy bar. He found a metal rod, but it was too wide to fit through the crack. He shoved it into the door, splintering little bits of wood off the side of the beams, but making no concrete progress. Every noise felt so loud.

Outside, thunder rumbled louder and a long gust of wind moaned through the open windows of the tower. There was a bright flash of light and Tomkin waited for the next peal of thunder. When it happened, he shoved at the door as hard as he could, the noises he made drowned out by the rumbling storm.

The door didn't move.

At the next thunderclap, Tomkin let out a yell and slammed against it, barely making it quiver.

Why couldn't anything go right today? Tomkin pounded his fist against the door, against the fact that he was trapped, against the reality that there was actually a dragon here.

"Is there anything I could assist you with?" a gravelly voice said from behind him.

Tomkin whirled around to find Wink sitting smugly on Mags' chair, his short feet dangling far above the floor. "Where's Mags? Is she okay?"

"She's just fine."

"Did the dragon trap her somewhere else?"

"She has never been trapped here. I believe she has explained that to you several times."

"She was locked in this tower!"

The kobold shrugged. "I can open the door at any time."

Tomkin stopped. "You *what*?"

"You don't know much about kobolds, do you? I can manipulate and fix anything I find around me. I can put rocks back where they are supposed to be." He waved his long, knobby fingers at a small pile of rubble and it flew into the air, tucking itself neatly into a long crack in the wall and leaving it looking new. "I can reform wood back to its original condition." He gestured at the crescent of floor above him and a sagging beam along the edge began to straighten.

Tomkin stared at it. "That's amazing! I thought kobolds were only good for cleaning or fixing little things."

"Most ignorant people do."

"Is it hard? Mags said it takes a lot out of you."

Wink appraised the ceiling above him. "Fixing that completely would take most of the day. And it would be tiring."

"Can you destroy things too? Or shrink them?"

"Destroying and shrinking are simple." Wink motioned to a rock on the floor and it shrank to a pebble. "And takes almost no energy at all."

"Astonishing! Can you change more than one thing at a time?"

Wink gave the smallest hint of a smile at Tomkin's enthusiasm. "It depends on how related they are. I can't alter both this piece of wood and that piece of iron at the same time. But these," he lined up five broken pieces of wood on the desk, "were all part of the same plank of wood—"

"How can you tell?"

Wink scowled at the interruption. "Because they're all hickory wood with the same grain, density, and sap distribution, if you must know."

Tomkin stared at the little kobold. "You can just...sense that?"

Wink shrugged. Then he waved his hand over the pieces

of wood and each one began to swell slightly. "So I could expand all of them at once. Of course, it's much easier to make them shrink than expand." With another wave, each piece of wood began to shrink until they were just a handful of splinters.

"That is truly amazing," Tomkin said, picking up one of the pieces.

A little smile softened Wink's face.

"Really, you should leave Mags and come somewhere you could be useful." Tomkin looked around the tower. "There's no point in fixing up this place just for crazy old Mags."

Wink's smile vanished and his mouth pressed into a small, thin line.

"Anyway, did Mags make you come here to get me out?" Tomkin asked.

His lips drew even thinner. "I make my own decisions."

"You do?" Tomkin studied the kobold. "I thought you had to do whatever she said."

"I think it's safe to assume you know nothing about me. I choose to serve her because she is good and honorable. I am not her slave, and she does not treat me like one."

Tomkin decided not to say anything about that. "You offered to help me. Were you serious?"

Wink paused. "I was."

Tomkin looked at him for a long moment. Wink stared back at him, eyebrows raised and a benign smile on his face.

"Can you open the door?"

"I can. I'm just not sure I want to."

"Why on earth not?"

"You do know there's a dragon out there, right?"

"Of course I know there's a dragon out there. That's the whole reason I'm here."

"Do you intend to kill it?"

Tomkin paused. That was the question. If the opportunity

arose, of course, but those scales and the sheer size of it… "No."

Wink cocked his head slightly. "Why not?"

Tomkin paused again. He wasn't going to kill the dragon because there was no way on earth he could even injure it, much less kill it. But Wink wouldn't want to hear about going back home to get reinforcements. Because there was no way Tomkin was going to let a dragon get cozy in Marshwell, especially in a fortified castle.

"I…," Tomkin began. "I admit I hadn't considered the dragon wouldn't just eat everyone it saw." That was true. "Maybe Mags is right about it." Except she wasn't. "Maybe the dragon isn't what I expected it to be." Except it was.

Wink narrowed his enormous brown eyes.

Tomkin tried not to squirm. Kobolds couldn't read minds, could they? Tomkin gave the little creature a weak smile.

A crack of thunder shook the tower at the same moment a flash of lightning lit the windows above them. Tomkin jumped, but Wink didn't move.

"My mistress is always right," Wink said. "But I've decided to help you, even if you can't quite see that she is." He smiled a wide smile. "Here you go."

There was a shifting noise outside the door and Wink began to fade until all Tomkin could see was a long pointy nose and an eerie smile. Then the kobold was gone. Uneasiness pricked Tomkin's gut. That had been too easy.

Behind him, the door swung open.

CHAPTER NINE

THE DOOR CREAKED, nudged by a blustery wind.

"Thank you," Tomkin said to the empty tower behind him. "I think."

He leaned out and peered in awe at the world outside. The sun had fallen behind the cliff soaring up next to the castle, which should have filled the courtyard with shadows. But the front edge of the storm, rolling westward and gobbling up the blue sky before it, blazed with reds and yellows. The reflected light bathed the castle in a warm orange glow.

Tomkin pulled his eyes from the mesmerizing sight. Wind blustered this way and that, sending leaves and dust scuttling about. Across the bailey, as Mags would call it, which was not large enough to deserve such a name, a squat, square tower stood. It was a little shorter than the round tower he was standing in, but much wider.

To his left, an opening in the ground led to the stairway below, to where he had first encountered the dragon. The bailey and the two towers were encircled by a wall twice Tomkin's height. To his right, the barred castle gate stood between him and the stairs to his little boat. Except for the swirling wind, the courtyard was still. Cautiously, he took a few steps out of the doorway, toward the gate.

Something white plummeted out of the sky and landed in front of him with a sickening thud. It took Tomkin's mind one long, horrified moment to realize it was the broken body of a lamb. He jumped back against the wall just as a rush of orange scales, searingly bright against the darkening skies, streaked down and landed, curling neatly into the bailey.

The sheep lay twisted and still on the stones. Tomkin's gaze flicked between the viciousness of the dragon and the brokenness of the lamb. The bailey had felt small before the dragon filled it, but now it was a prison cell surrounded by stone and storm and filled with death.

Tomkin didn't breathe, the dragon didn't stir.

Vorath's lazy gaze ran across Tomkin before pointing his snout toward the sheep and blowing out a stream of fire. The wool lit and burned. It sizzled and curled back from the flame, shrinking into dark, brittle-looking beads. The wind caught tendrils of smoke and Tomkin gagged at the stench of burning hair.

When the sheep was covered with nothing but ashes and pellets of burned wool, the dragon picked it up and shook it until it was bare.

Vorath dropped the sheep in front of Tomkin, pinning its back legs with long black claws. Tomkin looked away from the sheep to find Vorath staring at him. His horrible orange snout drew closer, stretched open to reveal a gaping maw, then snapped shut on the front of the sheep and ripped it in two.

Tomkin squeezed his eyes shut against the torn sheep and the dragon's flat gaze. He pushed back tighter against the wall, waiting to feel the claws, the teeth, tear into his own body. The air smelled again of hot metal and stone. Of fire and destruction. And now there was the tang of blood.

Please don't eat me, please don't eat me. The words spun through his mind over and over.

I'm not going to eat you. Vorath's voice sounded inside Tomkin's head.

Tomkin froze. Vorath could read his mind! He paused. No, maybe not. Anyone in Tomkin's position would be thinking about being eaten. The dragon had turned back to the sheep. Tomkin focused on the dragon and thought as loud as he could, *CAN YOU READ MY MIND?*

The dragon flinched. *Do not shout.* His voice cracked like a whip.

Sorry. Tomkin's mind felt clunky. *Can you hear all my thoughts?*

The ones you shout.

Stuffing his thoughts very low, he whisper-thought, *I don't know how to think quietly.*

Vorath snorted. *Not many humans do.*

The dragon grabbed the last shred of sheep, tossed it into the air, and snapped his jaws closed around it with a crunch. Then Vorath turned back to Tomkin.

The scent of the burned wool blew past again and Tomkin coughed. It smelled terrible. Why would Vorath want to eat near that smell?

Unburned wool tastes worse.

Tomkin grimaced at the idea of a mouthful of wool.

Who are you? Vorath asked. *I do not think the sword is yours. Did you steal the livery of Marshwell as well? Are you a common thief?*

Tomkin shoved himself off the wall. "My father is the Duke of Marshwell and these are my colors. I wear them every day."

Ahh, the Dukeling has a spine. Maybe he deserves the colors, even if he does not deserve the sword.

"And that sword belongs to my family. I have as much right to wield it as anyone."

But not as much skill. The dragon regarded Tomkin for a long moment.

Tomkin watched the dragon's nostrils expand and contract with each breath. Its yellow eyes watched him, intelligent and emotionless. He didn't attack, didn't threaten, just looked at Tomkin as though weighing him.

Maybe Mags was right. Maybe this dragon wasn't as bad as he'd thought.

"Why haven't you eaten me?" Tomkin whispered.

Vorath's head cocked ever so slightly. *Why would I waste your death here? Where no one would witness it?*

Tomkin's heart sank. Maybe this dragon was worse. "And the girl? What have you done with her?"

You do understand that dragons feel differently about maidens than they do about... The dragon took in and dismissed all of Tomkin in a tiny shifting of expression. *...knights.*

"Dragons eat maidens. Everyone knows this."

Vorath snorted out a shot of smoke. *What I do with the girl is none of your concern.*

Tomkin's pulse quickened. Mags was still alive.

Vorath dropped his head until it skimmed the ground in front of Tomkin. He moved closer until Tomkin could see each tiny scale overlapping its neighbor, forming an impenetrable armor wrapped around the dragon's face. The orange scales rippled as he moved. The dark nostrils breathed out forge-hot air. But the yellow eyes were the worst—torrid and poisonous.

I have not eaten you yet, he said, his voice quiet and impassive, *because it is more useful to wait. But do not worry, little Dukeling, I will not make you wait past tomorrow morning.*

The words sent a chill into Tomkin's chest. He stepped away from the dragon and felt the cold wall against his back.

The dragon glanced around the courtyard. *You are freed from the tower,* he said, as though granting permission instead of stating the obvious. *That is acceptable. There is no way out of this fortress. Do not kill yourself trying to escape before I have the pleasure of killing you myself.*

The dragon turned its head away from him and slithered smoothly, serpentinely, to the stairs leading below the bailey. With a motion as fluid as blazing orange water, the dragon slipped down the stairs to return to the great hall where it slept.

Mags was wrong. The dragon was evil. Tomkin had to find her and get them both away from here.

CHAPTER TEN

Tomkin slid along the wall until something caught at his sleeve and the shoulder ripped open. Startled, he jerked away from the wall, expecting to see fangs, but finding only a broken nail. With a glance around the empty bailey, he ran to the gate. A thin set of stairs set into the wall next to him led to the top. He ran up them and looked over.

The rain was getting closer, marching across the hills toward him. The most distant were already lost behind a grey veil. A crack of lightning split the air. Thunder shook the wall and Tomkin felt it vibrate in his chest.

He tore his eyes away from the storm and looked below him. From the gate, ragged, broken steps wound down the cliff face to the river. He could just see the half-submerged dock at the base of them.

But no boat.

Where was it? Something shifted near the next bend of the Great River. Against the far side, his little rowboat floated— burning. As he watched, the last of the blackened wood slid down under the water.

He stared at the spot for a long moment, as though the boat was going to bob up and paddle itself upstream to the dock. Of course Vorath would have destroyed the boat. The river was the only way out of here.

The water blurred, and it took him a moment to realize the rain had arrived at last. One fat drop landed on the wall next to his hand, splashing a tiny spray of cold water against him.

Then the real rain hit. Except rain was too feeble a word for it. Torrent. Deluge. It was a water giant climbing up, in one easy step, from the river to the castle, and flooding it.

In the time it took him to race back down the stairs to the small shelter of the recessed gate, Tomkin was soaked through. He pressed himself into the space under the wall. The wind arrived with a howl. More than a howl—a battle cry. Water and wind yanked Tomkin forward, then shoved him back against the gate.

He made a mad dash across the bailey back to the doorway of the keep. It was terrifically loud inside the tower, the downpour thrumming on the roof like a drum.

Tomkin strained to see across the courtyard. The rain formed a solid grey wall between him and the other tower, as if the water giant was stomping its rain-feet, trying to knock the castle off the cliff. Through a window of the square tower, a faint golden light flickered.

Mags—and she had a fire.

Lightning cracked, hitting the cliff behind the castle. The thunder wasn't a sound as much as a sundering of the skies. Tomkin ducked, half expecting a portion of the cliff to split off and crush him.

He had to get to Mags. He hurried along, staying close to the tower wall. Along the back of the castle, he ducked into a recess with an arrow-slit window. Peering through it he could see a bit of the lake behind the castle. The waterfall feeding it was sending down torrents of water. A half-submerged dock sat at the edge of the lake, and the thinnest line of a trail led away from it. Tomkin ran to the next window.

Lightning flashed again and an image was seared into his eyes: the path continued, scratching its way up the cliff face.

There was a way out besides the river!

Without another thought, he rushed across the bailey to the square tower and to Mags. It took twenty steps to reach the doorway. He darted through into safety.

Except inside the tower was just as rainy as outside. He jumped back into the shelter of the doorway. The roof of the square tower was almost completely missing, only the far corner was still intact. Huddled in that far corner, the roof above her being rebuilt by Wink, sat Mags, curled up before a feeble fire.

Tomkin paused in the thick doorway, where he was protected from the rain. Behind him the courtyard was still deluged. Ahead of him the interior of the tower was the same. There was a stretch along the far wall, where Mags was huddled, where the rain fell less. The bit of ceiling above her provided a sliver of dryness, but there wasn't enough room for Tomkin to fit.

He felt a pang of pity for the girl hunched in the corner. Couldn't she see that if the dragon was kind, he'd have invited her into the great hall? It was warm and dry and enormous. There was more than enough room for Mags and her imaginary court.

Instead, she had squeezed into a tiny ball, with her side pressed against the wall, next to a fire so small it was more like a candle sputtering in the corner. Wink stood beside her, peering at the roof.

The beam of wood above Mags straightened and grew.

The jagged shards of wood along its edge aligned themselves with each other and spread like a ripple across the surface of a pond, out and out until they reached the next beam, which was doing the same. The sheltered area around Mags grew until it covered most of the far corner of the tower. Wink sagged back against the wall. Mags stood and went to him, putting her arm around his shoulder and bringing him near the fire.

Tomkin looked at her in surprise. She was clean. Wink must have made her a new dress from the strands he'd taken from the rug. Her filthy clothes were gone and she wore a dark, warm-looking dress. Her face, cleaned of the dirt, was prettier than he'd expected. It might be because she was looking kindly at Wink instead of glaring at Tomkin, but she had a nice face.

Mags was a mystery. What on earth had made her come here? What had made her think a truce with a dragon was better than wherever she had come from? She clearly loved her father and sister. And her mother…

Tomkin's mind skirted away from the idea of losing his own mother. His parents were the steadiest people in the world. If his mother had been home when the news of the dragon came this morning, she would have come up with some rational plan that would have worked. Vorath would be taken care of by now, with Tomkin safely at home. In fact, by now his mother would have taken care of the dragon, drafted a plan to restore Colbreth Castle to its original grandeur, and planned Tomkin's wedding.

Mags and Wink settled down side by side with their backs to him, facing the small fire. Wink must have done something more, because within a few seconds the fire grew larger, lighting the corner and casting large, flickering shadows toward Tomkin. The homey smell of smoke drifted over to him.

The world around him was sliding into night, moving from grey to darker grey. Wink had fixed enough of the ceiling that there was room for Tomkin in their corner, but he paused in the doorway, shivering in his wet clothes. The rain fell behind him and in front of him, separating him from Mags and Wink by a moving, living mass of water and wind.

He held back, feeling strangely uninvited into the small

circle of Mags, Wink, and the cheery fire. Mags laughed, the sound breaking through the rain just enough for him to hear. She was gesturing to the walls and ceiling.

The rain slowed from downpour to heavy rain, and still Tomkin lingered. It would take a matter of seconds to dash across the square tower and reach the warmth of Mags' fire. Mags voice was audible over the rain now, and Tomkin shifted. Standing here any longer would turn him to an eaves-dropper. The thought of her turning to find him, listening from the darkness, was enough to break his stillness.

Tomkin stepped into the tower, staying against the wall to his right were the rain was lighter, and scooted towards Mags.

"You think this is a mistake?" she asked.

"No," Wink answered, "I'm saying the dragon is clever. You need to be more so if you're going to make this work. The dragon will keep you as long as it needs me to complete the castle. But after that...."

"So you don't think it means to be...friends." She had tried to make the question sound flippant, but it was tinged with disappointment. A deeper disappointment than Tomkin expected.

He paused, feeling intrusive. He'd expected to find them discussing castle renovations. He should cough, or scuff his foot, or make his presence known.

"I think he is more dragon than you want him to be," Wink said matter-of-factly, but not unkindly. "I'm afraid in this one instance, the boy is right."

"Argh!" Mags dropped her head into her hands. "Him! Of all the knights or warriors who could have shown up to fight Vorath, why did it have to be Tomkin Thornhewn, youngest son of the Duke of Marshwell?"

Tomkin shrank back against the wall, indignance and embarrassment warring inside him.

"Why can't they just go away?" she asked. "We could make this castle great. I could be happy here in a place I choose, instead of being forced into a place the world chooses for me.'

Tomkin began to creep back toward the door.

"I know, child," said the kobold. "But they are both here, and while Marshwell might object to you staying here, the more pressing issue is the dragon. You need to convince him you are more valuable to him alive. You need to tell him who you are."

Tomkin hesitated.

"It feels a bit awkward to introduce myself now."

"Awkward is better than dead," Wink pointed out.

"I don't think it will help."

"Yes it will. Because whether you like it or not, you are valuable to a good many people. If the dragon can recognize the value of the boy from Marshwell, he'll recognize you are worth even more."

Tomkin froze. She was...what?

"Your holding is larger than Marshwell. If your families allied, then Vorath would face a large enough force that it would be difficult for him. He will realize he needs you on his side."

Tomkin looked hard at Mags. Her holding was larger than Marshwell? There were only two in all of Queensland. North Peak was on the far northern border, days away. That left only...

Tomkin's stomach sank down to the flagstone floor.

Mags sighed. "I don't want to be me any longer."

Wink set his long, knobby hand on Mags' shoulder. "You can't become someone new without making peace with who you already are."

"I'm glad you're here, Wink," Mags said softly.

"Always, my lady."

Tomkin stepped out into the rain, barely feeling it. His

mind spun. The only other holding larger than Marshwell was…Greentree.

Mags stood and drew herself up as tall as she could. "I'll go to Vorath and say, 'Hello, I need to introduce myself. My name is—'"

Tomkin marched into their firelight. "Lissa of Greentree!"

CHAPTER ELEVEN

MAGS WHIRLED TOWARD TOMKIN, her hand flying to her mouth.

"You are *Lady Lissa*? Of *Greentree*?" This was the woman he was supposed to marry? *This*?

Tomkin stomped toward her, until she had to step back.

"You *lied* to me!" he declared.

Mags dropped her hand and stepped forward, straight as an arrow. "I did *not* lie to you. I just didn't tell you who I am."

"Lies don't always involve words."

Her eyes narrowed and she glared at him. "Well, why should I tell you? We're not friends."

Tomkin glared at her with equal fury. "No. We are not friends. Nor will we ever be. It's nice to know I was right about you, even before I met you. I didn't find a castle with one dragon, I found a castle with two."

Mags' face filled with disgust. "You have no idea how insulted I was that my father matched me with the youngest son of someone as insignificant as the Duke of Marshwell. Marshwell!"

Tomkin stared at her angry face. He'd been worried about her. He had tried to rescue her. When all this time she had been here because she was running away from *him*. She had chosen living with a dragon over marrying him.

"Your land is a stinking swamp," she continued, stepping forward until she was almost touching him. She stood glaring up at him like a little ball of fire. "And you are such an insignificant part of it, that were I to marry you, we'd probably end up crammed together in a mud hut stuck in the middle of your 'mournful' marshes. Which would fit, because having to spend my life with you would be worth mourning."

"You're in Marshwell right now," Tomkin said, gritting his teeth and motioning to the castle and the cliffs and the river. "Do you see any marshes? Marshwell is a beautiful place."

Mags gave the pouring rain behind him a disgusted glance. "Yes, it's lovely here."

"You tried to steal this castle to make it your home! How did you think that was going to work? Do you think you can just saunter into Marshwell, flip your soaking wet hair around, and declare something yours? This isn't Greentree. Here, you are nobody. I can kick you out of here at any moment."

"Like you can kick out the dragon?"

He leaned forward until he was looking down into her furious face. "I'd rather have the dragon."

Mags gave him a withering look. "You and your family left this castle in ruins. I'm not taking anything from anyone. You already threw it away."

"Well I'm claiming it again for Marshwell." Tomkin grabbed the torn sleeve of his shirt, right above Marshwell's shield, and yanked. The sleeve tore off easily and he peeled it off his arm. It flipped inside out in the process and he tugged at the wet fabric, swearing and grunting at it, trying to turn it the right way.

Mags crossed her arms and raised one eyebrow.

With a final snap of the fabric, Tomkin flipped it the right way, grabbed a thin piece of wood off the floor, and tied the sleeve to it. This was his castle and no spoiled girl was going to take it. He marched over to a nearby window and jabbed the piece of wood into a crack between the rocks. When he let go, the stick sagged to the side, the sleeve hanging limp and soaked against the side of the window. It looked pathetic.

Tomkin spun back towards her. "Colbreth Castle belongs to Marshwell."

Mags eyed the makeshift flag with contempt. There was a scraping noise behind him. He glanced over his shoulder to see the stick, weighed down by the wet sleeve, tip over and fall out the window.

"Take it up with Vorath," Mags said.

A gust of wind blew into the tower and Tomkin's bare arm felt even colder than the rest of him. He glared at her. "I came here to tell you I found us a way out."

"I don't *want* a way out."

"You can't be serious about that. The dragon is going to kill you. Maybe not tonight, maybe not tomorrow, but when he is done with you, he will kill you."

Mags took a deep breath, then looked at Tomkin like he was a child. "I understand you don't want to be here. I do not understand your misguided attempt to save me. I release you from whatever obligation you feel you are under." Her voice softened and took on a pleading tone. "You should go. Get out tonight, because you're obviously going to make Vorath mad, and I don't want to be the reason you stayed and died."

She gestured toward the night. "Just leave this castle and leave us alone. You haven't cared about this place for generations. Don't start now. I'll talk to Vorath about getting his own flock of sheep and then he won't need to hunt from anyone in your land. We'll live happily here and you can live happily far away."

Mags turned away from him and went back to the fire, picking up a piece of wood and tossing it on. She held her hands out to it. Wink positioned himself next to her, his back turned as well.

Tomkin stood, shivering. He couldn't just leave her, as much as he wanted to. He couldn't walk away and let her kill herself.

"What am I supposed to tell your father?" he asked her quietly.

Mags' back stiffened and she turned, eyes glinting. "You don't have to tell my father anything. I will explain it to him myself."

Tomkin's temper flared. "Fine. Wink, try not to get killed also. When all this is over and we are searching for your mistress's bones, I'd like a witness to the fact that I did everything besides throw her over my shoulder and carry her out of here like the child she is." He whirled around to go.

The hair on his arm and neck stood up, sending a tingling feeling across his shoulders. With a blinding flash, lightning hit the roof of the tower. The concussion of thunder was not a sound, it was a force. Like the water giant pounding his colossal fist into Tomkin's chest.

A scattering of rocks landed around him and Tomkin ducked back against the wall. He looked up in time to see a large stone plummeting towards him.

Even the castle is trying to kill me.

Pain split his head with a flash brighter than the lighting, dropping him to his knees. The edges of the tower blurred and darkness rushed over him.

The next thing Tomkin knew, he was lying on the hard ground, his arms and legs too heavy to move. When he opened his eyes, the light of the fire stabbed into them. He groaned, squeezed them closed, and turned his head away. Pain shot into his skull.

"Stay still." Mags' voice came too loud next to his ear.

Something touched the back of his head and the pain took his breath away. He tried to pull away, but a hand stopped him.

"Stay still," she said firmly.

He wanted to tell her to stop touching him, but his mouth didn't seem to want to do anything but groan.

"If you'd stop making that noise," Mags said, "it would be nice."

Tomkin groaned again, putting a little extra effort and volume into it.

"Oh, stop." He was jostled, his head lifted and set back down on something soft. Which was nice. Damp, but nice. Something warm started to stroke through his hair. Warm and wet.

He cracked his eyes open again. Next to the fire, Wink peered into a copper cup.

Tomkin shifted, stretching his legs a little. Another burst of pain lanced through his skull. He lifted his hand, still a little heavier and clumsier than it should be, to feel his head.

"Don't touch," Mags said and batted his hand away.

"Why not?" Tomkin demanded. Except it sounded more plaintive than demanding.

"Because you crashed your head into a rock and you shouldn't touch it. You'll be fine—at least I think you will—but you shouldn't touch it. I'm trying to clean it up, and you need to leave it alone."

"I didn't crash my head into a rock! A part of the tower fell off and smashed into me!"

"Is there a difference?"

The world shifted and he saw Mags hand something to Wink over his head. It was a small, dark red rag. Wink dropped it in the copper cup. He wrung it out and handed it back to her, not nearly as red.

"Is that my blood?" Tomkin shoved at the ground, trying to sit up.

"Of course it's your blood." Mags pressed firmly on his shoulder, immobilizing him. "You ran your head into a rock. Now lay still so I can clean it up. There's an awful lot in your hair."

He wanted to protest. Actually, he wanted to tell Mags he hated her, but her arm had been so freakishly strong and the wet rag, almost hot, felt so good on his head, he settled for a scowl.

She was Lissa of Greentree. His betrothed, technically.

"You lied to me."

The rag paused, then continued stroking through his hair. If that rag hadn't been connected to Lying Lissa, it might have been soothing. And if there weren't stabs of pain each time she came too close to the wound.

"I didn't lie." Her voice was prim.

"You knew who I was," Tomkin accused her, and this time it almost came out accusing, except for the slight slur.

The rag continued stroking across his hair, but it was getting colder. She passed it to Wink again before answering.

"I came here because I am done being Lissa of Greentree." The rag came back hot. "I had no intention of telling anyone my name. It doesn't do much good to run away from your life and then tell the first person you meet who you are."

There was a logic to that. It was a stupid logic, but he had nothing to say to it. He hadn't wanted to marry her—and now he knew he needed to find a way to get his father to end the betrothal—but he wouldn't have lied to her about who he was. "What exactly was so terrible about being you? The fact you were betrothed to the second son of a lesser duke?" His voice had cracked a little at the end, and he clamped his mouth shut, putting more emphasis on his scowl.

The rag stopped and Mags' arm rested on Tomkin's shoulder.

That was the moment he realized his head was in her lap. In her lap! He shoved himself off of her.

Pain split his skull and flashes of light arced across his vision. He grabbed at his head, just as Mags' shrill voice stabbed into his ears.

"Don't be stupid. Lay down until you feel better."

He shoved her hands away and leaned back against the wall, focusing on the fire that kept slipping sideways. The castle bucked under him like a living creature.

Tomkin focused on the feeling of the solid wall behind him and waited for the world to stop shifting. A gust of wind blew past, brushing chilly fingers across Tomkin's neck. His head throbbed from his shivering.

"Oh, come on," Mags said, exasperated. "Let's move you closer to the fire. I didn't do all that work to your head just to have you freeze to death."

CHAPTER TWELVE

MAGS STOOD in front of him and offered her hand. He wanted to refuse, just because it was Mags offering, but he was too cold. He took her hand and rose to his feet. The fire slid to the left again, in a crooked, tipping sort of way, and Mags shoved her shoulder under his arm.

"Don't fall. You'll hit your head again. This way, just a few steps."

The two of them stumbled to the corner, and Mags sort of helped, sort of hindered, as he sank down against the wall. The stones this close to the fire were warm on his back. Tomkin drew his knees up and rested his chin on them, looking into the flames and absorbing the warmth.

Mags went to the corner and came back with a little bowl of nuts. She sat next to him, offering the bowl. He glanced around for Wink, but the kobold must have disappeared off to...wherever kobolds disappeared to.

"You're still shivering." Mags gave a tiny, annoyed sigh, then scooted next to him. He wanted to be annoyed right back at her, but she was so warm.

Tomkin stared into the fire and munched on the nuts,

trying not do anything that would hurt his head. Like moving, or thinking.

"Coming here had nothing to do with marrying you," Mags said quietly.

Tomkin stared into the fire. "You've made it clear how you feel about Marshwell and youngest sons. Don't try to apologize for it now."

"I'm not apologizing," she said. "I don't want to marry you any more than you want to marry me. But that's not why I didn't tell you who I was, and it's not why I left Greentree."

"Who do you want to marry?" he asked. It was a sullen, sulky question, and he was annoyed at himself for asking.

"I don't want to marry anyone," she snapped. "At least not anyone I know. I just want to have a home that is mine and that I can run. Greentree is massive. Do you have any idea what it takes to run a holding like that?"

Tomkin's head throbbed and Mags' voice kept stabbing into the pain. He was trying to follow what she was saying, but mostly he wished she would just stop talking.

"I didn't mean to sound so…mean about Marshwell," Mags' voice was quieter, thank the skies. "I don't have anything against it. The parts I've seen are pretty. And it's insignificant enough that I wouldn't be required to do things like visit court every year."

Tomkin ignored the "insignificant" part.

"I'd forgotten Greentree goes to court," Tomkin said. A memory nagged at him. The pain was receding now that Mags was done being shrill. And the fire was so warm. Some part of his brain was telling him to stop talking, that he was about to say something he shouldn't. It sounded suspiciously like some sort of long-bearded mentor, the kind that shows up in all the old stories, directing the hero onto the right path. But the bearded voice was tucked pretty far back, and whatever part was feeding words to his mouth seemed unhindered by it.

With the corner behind them and the wall of rain like a dark, rustling curtain at the edge of the firelight, it was like they sat in a haven of calm, separated from the rest of the world.

"You know Princess Ellona, don't you?" Tomkin asked. "I hear she's the most beautiful girl in Queensland."

Mags snorted.

Tomkin glanced at her. "Isn't she?"

"Oh yes, she's lovely." The look on Mags' face was so venomous, Tomkin pulled away from her.

The memory clicked into place. "Oh, right. You don't get along with the princess, do you? Didn't you do something horrible to her? Slap her face in front of the court, or something stupid like that?"

"Slap her face!" Mags' shrill voice pierced into Tomkin's head and he doubled over, slapping his hands over his ears.

Obviously, that wasn't the right story. But it was something like that. That's where Mags'd got her Dragon nickname...maybe.

Past his hands, Mags' voice screeched on.

"Mags!" He interrupted her.

She whirled on him. "My name is Lissa!"

"Well I'm less annoyed with Mags than I am with Lissa of Greentree," he shot at her, keeping his head ducked and his ears covered, "so I'm sticking with Mags. And will you *please* lower your voice? You normal voice is almost soothing. But when you yell, it's like a tiny man pounding an axe into my skull."

She was silent. Tomkin turned to look at her and found her face such a mess of emotions he didn't know how to interpret it.

Her eyes were unusually bright. Did they normally look like that? Maybe it was the fire. They were pretty. Light brown. And so shiny.

She blinked and the shine disappeared.

"Are you crying?"

The bearded old man voice in his brain threw his hands up in the air in despair. Tomkin paused. He blinked a few times, trying to clear the fog. He sat straighter and took some deep breaths while he ran back over the low points of their conversation.

He grimaced. "I'm sorry, Mags. My brain isn't working quite right. I'm not usually this…."

"Thick?" she offered, but her voice was lower, and her scowl had loosened a little.

Tomkin let out a short laugh. Thick was just the word. "I had no right to say anything about you and the princess. I have no idea what happened there. It was just rumors and I hate when people spread rumors about me." His mouth was running a little faster than he was comfortable with, but a glance at Mags' face showed her scowl was almost gone, so he let it run. "Last summer my brother was home for a short time between skirmishes on the border."

Mags nodded. "I've met your brother. He was really…tall."

Tomkin sighed. "That's Elton." Of course she had met Elton. Tallest man in any room, shoulders like an ox, looked like a hero who'd just stepped from the pages of a storybook. Tomkin knew very well how he looked to someone who had met Elton. "Everyone loves Elton."

Mags was quiet for a moment. "He seemed like a fine person. A little too knight-in-shining-armor for me, though."

Tomkin glanced at her, but she was studying the fire. "Really?"

She shrugged. "I've never been a fan of the giant warrior type."

He almost asked what type she was a fan of, but the bearded voice slapped his teeth shut. It pointed him back to the topic of rumors.

"There aren't too many people my age at the holding,"

Tomkin began. "Anyone over ten works in the pea grain fields. There are at least a dozen maids, but several years ago the head housemistress gave them all uniforms with bulky black dresses and black scarfy things that cover their hair. Honestly, I can't tell them apart anymore. It wouldn't matter if I could, though, because they're instructed not to talk to me. And if I try, they just giggle and run away."

"That sounds lonely," Mags said quietly.

Tomkin stared hard at the fire. It was lonely, but that wasn't what he had intended to say. Maybe none of this was what he had intended to say.

Past the fire, the rain fell in a dark, shushing wall.

"Do you like your brother?" Mags asked. She sounded genuinely curious.

"I love my brother. We don't quarrel much. But Elton's five years older than me. He was trained to fight when we were young. He was a natural at it. He's built like my father.

"I'm more like my mother. And though they trained me a bit when I was younger, I wasn't strong enough to do much. By the time I was, the skirmishes with Coastal Baylon had begun and my father, brother, and every worthwhile fighting man were stationed along the border. There was no one left to teach me anything.

"My mother needed help running the holding." Tomkin shrugged. "She says I've got a knack for it. These days I do most of the hearing hours, when folks come to us with problems." He glanced at Mags. "Do you do that in Greentree?"

She nodded.

Tomkin waited a moment, but she said nothing more. Which was kind of her, really. It was only Tomkin who enjoyed solving the constant stream of petty problems the people of Marshwell brought during the hearing hours. His father and brother found any excuse to do something else. Mags probably did, too.

"Anyway, we were supposed to all go on a hunt, but we

got word that a lord from Coastal Baylon had sent troops into Marshwell.

"All the men raced off. I stayed back. My mother was ill and I couldn't leave her. Instead I called the Baylonian ambassador and demanded to know why they were inside our borders." Tomkin let the story hang for a moment. He had been furious that morning. Furious that the day with his brother was ruined. Furious that Baylon couldn't just leave well enough alone.

Whether it was his anger, or the fact that his mother wasn't there to take control of the negotiations, Tomkin had found himself in an unusual position of power. He'd worked with the ambassador for hours, probing and prodding, searching for whatever leverage was needed to get Baylon to leave Marshwell.

"It took all day before I figured out what they really wanted." At Mags' questioning look Tomkin rolled his eyes. "It all boiled down to sheep, if you'll believe that, a specific kind of wool the Baylonian lord's wife wanted." He stared into the fire. "But once you understand your enemy, then you can leverage what they want. From that point it was easy to come up with a treaty."

He glanced at Mags. "And I did. It was fair, cost Marshwell almost nothing, and secured that piece of border for the next decade."

Her eyebrows rose a little.

"None of that mattered, though, because that night the men returned. We heard them enter the courtyard and the ambassador and I went out to meet them." Tomkin sank back against the wall.

"Elton had slain the son of the Baylonian lord. That son turned out to be the ambassador's best friend. When he heard of the death he...went mad. He pulled out a knife and attacked me."

The ambassador had snarled like a rabid animal, something raw and frenzied in his eyes.

"I had spent the day working with him. He was intelligent and courteous, but when he heard of his friend's death... something snapped."

Mags nodded next to him and he glanced at her. Something in her face made him think she understood.

He looked back at the fire. "I was only holding a quill. I didn't even have a weapon. I was so surprised...I tried to get away from him but...I tripped and fell." His stomach twisted at the memory. "I thought I was dead." He took a deep breath. "But Elton jumped in and blocked him."

Tomkin sighed. "The treaty was ignored and that portion of our border has been the most violent ever since. But on top of that, everyone says the men went off to fight, while I hid at home. And when the little ambassador attacked, I tried to fight him with a quill."

He stopped and stared into the fire. Why had he said all that? He had never talked to anyone about that. The rumor had lingered. He knew it was a running joke among the workers at the holding. And probably throughout the rest of Marshwell as well.

Next to him, Mags was quiet. He shouldn't have told that story. She was already less than impressed with him. What if they did have to get married? He should have at least tried to keep her from thinking he was...whatever everyone else thought he was.

The silence between them stretched out. Tomkin felt himself shrinking against the stone wall. He wanted to break the silence, to pull the conversation away from how pathetic he was. But he could think of nothing to say.

It was Mags who finally spoke, her voice somehow lower than the rain and the crackle of the fire.

"I'm here because my mother died, and I can't bear to be a disappointment to my father any longer."

CHAPTER THIRTEEN

TOMKIN SAT VERY STILL. Something in his chest clenched at the sadness in her voice. It was a different sort of voice than he'd heard her use before. A more real voice. It was achingly lonely and broken and true. He started to look towards her, but didn't know what he'd see, and he didn't want her to misread anything in his expression, so he turned his eyes back to the fire.

"My mother died a little over a year ago. She caught the red cough from some village she had gone to, doing something kind and generous." The words *kind* and *generous* didn't sound kind or generous. "She died quickly, which was...I can't say *good*...but some people linger."

Tomkin opened his mouth to say something, anything, but what could someone say to that? He shut it again slowly.

Beside him he felt Mags take a deep breath. Her hands, wrapped around her knees, tightened slightly. "I tried, after she died, to take over her roles in Greentree.

"I always knew I wasn't like her. She was so thoughtful and unselfish and...wise. Everyone at the homestead loved her, from the lowest scullery girl to my father's chief advisor, because somehow she managed to make them each feel like they were just as important, just as valuable as she was."

Silence stretched out while the fire crackled and the rain thrummed down, steadier now, the urgency gone. The water giant must have moved on, wreaking destruction further west and leaving only his robe of rain trailing behind him.

"I don't know how she did it." Mags' voice was quiet enough to slip through the other noises. "I don't know how she was so patient all the time. I can't keep my mouth shut, I can't stop being irritated by petty things. I want to, but I can't. And it's so much worse since she died. I think she anchored me, somehow, in a better place than I can manage by myself. Or maybe she was such a buffer against the world, I could cling to her and her patience rubbed off on me."

Mags' thumb began to rub across her other fingers, worrying at them.

"I do go to court, sometimes. But I have only been once without my mother."

Tomkin opened his mouth to stop her, to tell her she didn't have to explain anything to him, but she rushed on.

"We were invited to the Spring Ball. My father had not been to court since my mother died, and he needed to go to the capital for the king's council anyway. There was tension between him and a couple other dukes who are closer to the king than he is. I knew he was nervous about it. He was afraid they might turn the king against Greentree if he wasn't there to defend himself.

"I didn't want to go, and he knew it. I believe my exact words to him were I didn't want to go to a stupid ball and spend the evening with stupid people. To convince me to come, he gave me one of my mother's gowns. It had been her favorite and my father'd had it altered to fit me. It was red. Not a gaudy red, a dark red, deep and steady. And I loved it."

She gave a little snort. "The princess wears light colors to the Spring Ball, so the other girls do as well. This one was going to stand out, and not in the way a girl wants to stand out at a ball. But my father's face, when he offered it to me...." Mags turned towards him. There was something in her face, something begging him to hear what she was saying.

She turned back to the fire. "My father never talks about my mother. I think it almost killed him to lose her. It may be killing him still.

"I hadn't seen it before she died, what she was to him. I knew they were happy, but happiness between two people is easy to dismiss as just normal, instead of being the most precious thing in the world. I hadn't realized that while I thought I needed her to stabilize me, without her, he is adrift. My father is a great man. But there's something in his face that wasn't there before. He's confused. Or lost.

"I took the dress and told him I would go."

Mags unclenched her hands and threw Tomkin a look that was somehow accusing. He had lost track of which things were his fault here, though, so the accusation just slid off of him.

"Your beautiful Princess Ellona is a hag. Want to know what a day spent with her is like? First, anyone who wants to be seen with her during the day must apply for it. No more than eight girls are chosen, the number depending on Ellona's plans for the day, and her mood. The chosen few must be up before dawn to have their clothing and hair approved." She ignored his raised eyebrow. "Then, they must all line up. Ellona comes in and ranks everyone based on clothing, general colors of hair and dress, and prettiness. You are then assigned a position. Those with positions one through three are allowed to be right at Ellona's side during the day. Everyone else must remain a certain distance away from her, depending on your rank."

"You can't be serious," Tomkin said.

"I usually rank around a six." She shot the number at him.

"A six? You're prettier than that!" He recognized he was

losing control of his words again, but they just kept coming. Besides, it was true. Ellona's logic made no sense and illogical things were annoying. "There can't be five girls prettier than you at court. I've seen noblemen's daughters. They're just as normal as any other girl. You look pretty here, all soggy and dirty. You must have looked even prettier at court."

Mags' expression froze for a moment, then softened. "Yes...well...thank you. But it's not good to be too pretty around Ellona. She picks girls who are just on the pretty edge of plain. She wouldn't consent to be seen with an ugly girl, unless she were especially rich, but she won't be seen with anyone she deems prettier than herself, either. You see, the Chosen Ones are used as ornament to her highness for the day.

"Ellona has long, flowing golden hair, of course. So to be close to her, you must have either dimmer golden hair, or dull brown hair. If Ellona is wearing green, then no one next to her can be in a clashing shade of green." Mags rolled her eyes. "And she's very sensitive about her nose, which is just fine, but she's convinced it's too big. So if you have a little nose"— Mags pointed to her own—"you're bound to get a low ranking.

"There's a political aspect to it, too. Since her retinue on any given day is made up of noblemen's daughters, they are almost always there for some reason that can be turned political. Ellona knows all of this and has an agenda. She's rude and asks insulting, personal questions in front of all the other girls in an effort to learn information that might help her father. And she's the princess, so you have to answer her. But if you do, she uses that information to begin rumors. Not just about you, it can be about your family, or your holding." Mags shook her head. "It's this terrible game of who can please Ellona more without actually giving away information she'll use against you. And she doesn't like girls who are too nice, so everyone stabs each other in the back just to try to please her." Mags shuddered. "It's terrible.

"The king is alright with this?" Tomkin demanded. "I thought he was a good man."

Mags shook her head. "I'm not sure the king understands what goes on. He adores her, you know. You can see it every time they're together. And when he is there, she is a different person. In fact, she is a different person everywhere but in these small groups of girls. He thinks the girls love Ellona so much, they tell her their secrets."

"Does your father know it's like that?"

Mags shook her head. "I've never told him. It's hard to believe about her when you're not right there. When I was *selected* last spring," her mouth twisted in a bitter smile, "I actually thought it was because Ellona felt sympathetic about my mother."

Silence fell between them again. Tomkin wanted to say something, but nothing in his mind sounded right. Mags' eyes were bright again, but her expression was so fierce the tears were probably afraid to fall.

"It was the second worst day of my life." Mags' voice was so low Tomkin leaned toward her. "Ellona began by telling me, and all the girls there, how much she had admired my mother. Because she was so simple and trusting and naive. And you just don't find that these days.

"She said all this sympathetically, of course. Everyone who walked by, which many people did, seeing as we sat in the center of the royal gardens, gazed at Ellona adoringly for how sweet she sounded. Because of course none of them actually listened to her. She pointed out how lucky my father was to have married above himself like he had, and how it was so sweet that he had fallen to pieces now that she was gone. How if my mother had still been alive, she would have stopped him from coming to court like a simpering fool."

Mags shot a sideways glance at Tomkin. "Then she began

to instruct me on the proper way to treat anyone under myself, because she'd heard I had a temper and she didn't want me alienating the workers at our home, now that I was in charge, however ineptly."

Tomkin locked his eyes on her shoes. That was all he'd ever heard about Lissa of Greentree, that she was rude to the help.

"It's not that I'm rude to people under me." There was something almost desperate in her voice and Tomkin had to look at her face. It was more bare than before. As though whether he believed her was the most important thing in the world. "There is no one above me at home, aside from my father. So it's not that I'm rude to people I see as beneath me." She looked miserably back at the fire. The next words came out barely above a whisper. "I'm just rude to everyone."

Tomkin bit his lip, hard. *This* was her revelation? He tried to keep the smile off his face, but it was no use. "Really?" Tomkin said. "I hadn't noticed."

Her eyes flashed at him, but seeing his expression, she stopped. "I don't mean to be." Her brows knit together. "It's just hard for me not to say what I'm thinking."

"I did notice that."

She glared at him, but there was less fury in it now.

He grinned at her. "I don't think it's a bad thing…entirely. Being honest is good."

"Then why does everyone hate me for it?"

This time Tomkin did laugh. "Because you make them feel terrible! Ellona was being honest, too. Or she would have said she was."

"Anyway," Mags said, scowling at him, "we hadn't brought any of our own ladies to court, it was just my father, me, and a couple of my father's men. So Ellona had provided a girl to help me with my clothes for the ball. The maid was horrible. Just as horrible as Ellona. And I was so tired from the day.

"I did try," she looked at Tomkin earnestly again. "I tried to ignore all her little 'compliments.' Ellona had trained her well, she knew all about my mother, my family, how my father was doing, the conflict going on with the other dukes. It was like some sort of nightmare. I couldn't get rid of her because I couldn't get dressed by myself.

"When I pulled out my mother's dress, she laughed. She asked if I intended to wear a blood-red dress to the Spring Ball. When I told her I was, she refused to help me put it on. She said Ellona wouldn't allow it, not on a girl who had been seen to be favored by her that day.

"I told her I didn't care what the she-devil Ellona wanted, and I was going to wear my mother's dress."

Mags stopped for a moment. She stared into the fire, her hands gripped together with white knuckles. When she continued, it was almost a whisper. "She picked up the dress and laughed. Said it was the ugliest thing she'd ever seen, too ugly for even an old woman like my mother to have liked. She said maybe my mother had died just so she'd never have to wear it again."

"What?"

"So I slapped her." Mags gave a broken, jagged laugh, before her face sobered. "She was still holding my dress and she was furious. She held it up in front of me and said, 'It looks like the seamstress missed something here in the bodice.' And she ripped the front of it apart."

Tomkin stared at her. "No."

Mags nodded. "A big, ragged tear right down the front. Then she left.

"Later there was a knock at my door. Ellona's voice came through asking if there was anything wrong. She had that sickeningly sweet tone again, just like she'd had all day while she insulted and manipulated everyone. She said she had a dress I could wear, since she'd heard mine had been damaged while traveling here."

"Damaged while traveling?"

Mags nodded "I was so furious, I opened the door and told her…Well, I told her I wasn't going to the ball."

Tomkin stared at her. Mags stared at her own fingers.

"*That's* what you said to her? You said worse things to me when I stepped too heavily on the floor of the keep."

She whirled on him. "That's because you were stomping around like a big, fat oaf!"

Tomkin smiled and raised an eyebrow. "See?"

Mags shot him a glance that started as a scowl, but soon a little smile crept into it. "What I really said was the only reason I would ever want to be near her again, was if there was a storm, I could hide under her nose and stay out of the rain."

Tomkin burst out laughing and Mags smiled wider.

"And then I told her my dearest wish was that someday, every one of the girls that were surrounding her would grow a backbone, just as I'd needed to, and tell the world how horrible she was. Especially the king. And I hoped one day, her outside would be as hideously ugly as her shriveled little soul." Mags gave a little lift to her chin.

Tomkin laughed hard enough his head started throbbing. "What did the other girls do?"

"I don't know. I wanted to slap Ellona so badly—I just slammed the door in her face. I hate that girl."

Tomkin held his head to try to stop the pain, even as he kept laughing. "I can see why. And I'm sorry I said anything about her."

Mags shrugged. "It's not your fault. Everyone loves Ellona. She keeps her circle of girls small so she can control them, and they're the only ones who know what she's really like."

"So she's the one who started the Dragon Lady Lissa name?" Tomkin guessed.

Mags winced. "I guess. Before the week was out the name had already reached Greentree."

"What did your father do? He didn't just stand by and let the name spread, did he?"

Mags shrank a little, her eyes pointed at the fire. "He probably thinks I deserve it."

"What?" Tomkin demanded. "You didn't tell him what happened?"

"He came by my room, furious. Ellona had told him I'd been acting petulant all day, and when she had sent a lady-in-waiting to help me prepare for the ball, I had slapped her and sent her away. Then I'd declared I didn't want to go to the stupid ball and spend the evening with the simpering fools who were only there to impress the king."

Tomkin sat very still.

"I'm sure he thinks I said that and I was talking about him, but those were Ellona's words. He was furious. Said Ellona had tried to cover for me, but the king had pulled the true story out of her. The king was not pleased. He'd told my father we were free to leave court, and he would send a messenger with his decisions regarding the other dukes." Mags picked up a stick and prodded the fire. "The king ruled against my father, of course, so he had to pay them a ridiculous sum of money."

"Did you tell him about the serving girl? And the dress?"

Mags shook her head. "You don't understand. My father can't even mention my mother without tears. I couldn't bear to tell him the dress was ruined.

"I've been trying to make it up to him ever since. But I just can't. I'm his oldest child and I've taken on more and more responsibility, but I know if I stay, I'll just do something like that again. I don't think I'm welcome at court any longer, and I don't think my father trusts me the way he used to. He's quieter and tells me less."

She stopped talking, and the sounds of the rain and fire

filled the silence. Tomkin sat still, not knowing what to say. It was Mags who finally spoke.

"So that is why I'm here. I had planned to leave home long before I heard I'd been betrothed to you. I know my father was just finding a way to get me out of Greentree, but honestly, a marriage to Marshwell isn't really good for our family. I'm guessing none of the more influential houses are willing to take me, seeing as how the king and Ellona don't like me.

"It had nothing to do with you, Tomkin. I didn't want my father to make a bad arrangement just to tuck me away somewhere out of sight. So I left. And now he can get on with doing the things Greentree needs, and maybe news will get to the capital and the king will approve of my disappearing."

CHAPTER FOURTEEN

THE RAIN HAD LESSENED, and by the time Mags was done it was, not gentle, exactly, but the fury had blown out of it.

Tomkin looked into the fire. "I think you should have told your father."

Mags rolled her eyes. "Of course I should have told him. But it's a little late now, don't you think? What's done is long done, and it's time to move on."

"You don't really think living here," Tomkin gestured around them to the crumbling walls and puddles, "is the answer to your problems, do you?"

Mags' lips drew into a thin line. "We're not talking about this again."

"I just think if you want to run away, pick someplace better. Go to the Scale Mountains. There are deserted forts and castles all over there from the years when Queensland and the nomads were at war. Surely you could find something there better than a ruined castle stuck halfway up a cliff and inhabited by a dragon." He tried to keep down his irritation. How could she think coming here—

Tomkin turned towards her. "How did you get here? Did

you come up from the river? I didn't see another boat. Do you know of another way in?"

Mags shuddered. "No, I didn't come by the river. I hate boats."

"What is there to hate about boats?"

"They sink. And then you drown." She seemed serious.

"Boats don't sink very often, and if they do, you just swim to shore."

She shook her head. "When I was little, there was this lake, and my foot got caught in the reeds at the bottom...." She clenched her eyes shut. "I don't like boats. I don't like water."

"You realize this castle is set between a lake and a river?"

She cracked her eyes open and Tomkin was surprised to see she was terrified.

"Okay." Remember not to talk to Mags about water. "Then how did you get here?"

"I rode on Vorath's back."

Tomkin's jaw dropped open. She had ridden on a dragon? Climbed on that scaly back and, what? Held on to his neck? She gave him a smug little smile.

"I met him across the river. I had been admiring this castle from the top of a hill, wondering how I was going to get to it without having to cross that horrid river, when Vorath flew out of the sky.

"I was so shocked, I froze. It was early in the morning and the hills were still in shadow, but he rose up into the sunlight and shone so bright, I thought he was on fire. He'd circled a time or two, lazy and effortless, before seeing me. When he did, he flew above me. He was so fluid, like a snake or an eel.

"I'll admit that was frightening," she looked at him earnestly. "But also beautiful. Mesmerizing."

Tomkin thought of the scales in the great room when he first saw the dragon. The ripples of dark and light fire that had raced across the scales while the dragon slept. He nodded.

"I knew he was going to eat me, of course, and it was a sad thought, in a very detached way. Because wonder and terror were both trying to take over and that didn't leave much room for a quiet little thing like sadness. But if this was going to be my end, I was at least going to meet it bravely."

He could picture her, tiny before the enormous dragon, her chin lifted, looking as imperiously at the dragon as she always did at Tomkin.

"I did have to clasp my hands together to keep them from shaking. He was bigger than I expected. He landed around me and curled himself into a circle, surrounding me. Then he just sort of looked at me."

Tomkin thought of the flat, yellow eyes staring. "He does that."

"I decided it couldn't hurt to be polite, so I greeted him with a formal curtsey. I was surprised when he talked to me with that think-talking he does." She cocked her head slightly. "Did you know he can talk? I forgot you were rude when you met him."

"Yes," Tomkin shuddered. "Echoes around my head, like I'm in a dark, creepy cavern."

"Your head is a lot like an empty cavern."

Tomkin whirled toward her. "It is not!"

She was smiling, the first real smile she'd directed at him. At his scowl, she laughed, a clear, bright sound.

"Vorath and I chatted for a bit. He asked if I had been looking for him, and I explained I was just looking for a nice home. I introduced Wink to him, too, who was *not* pleased to appear in front of a dragon. I don't know why, though, since he can blink out whenever he wants to."

"Where does he go when he does that?" Tomkin asked.

"Never far. Sometimes he just turns invisible and stays there. Or he can sort of hop about thirty paces in any direction in an instant. So he could have escaped easily enough. Vorath was very interested in him, of course.

"Eventually we agreed Vorath was in possession of a castle and I had the means to fix it, so maybe we should work together. You see, he only wants a place to live, unbothered by people. I pointed out that maybe I could get him his own herds, and we could keep them on the hills, which are almost entirely deserted. That way he wouldn't have angry farmers calling for his blood every time he got hungry."

"Are you going to shear his sheep for him, too?" Tomkin asked. "He doesn't like the taste of wool."

"I'm sure he can deal with that problem himself," Mags said primly. "You can tell from his eyes he's intelligent. He's quite lovely and friendly, too."

Tomkin felt another twang of pity for Mags. She believed what Vorath had said. He tried to keep his voice kind. "I saw Vorath before the storm began." Shutting his eyes to block out the memory of the torn sheep, the terrible crunch of Vorath's jaw, he continued, "He's going to kill me tomorrow morning Mags. Not here. I don't know where. Somewhere where it will be some sort of example."

Mags' eyes narrowed. "He told you that?"

Tomkin nodded. "He's intelligent. But he's not kind. He's just trying to manipulate you into helping him."

Mags turned away.

"Which is why we need to leave. I saw a trail going up the cliff. I think if we can find the way out the back of the castle by the lake, we can reach it and—"

"I'm *not* going with you." Mags crossed her arms. "Wink and I will be fine."

Tomkin glared at her stubborn face with its stubborn scowl and its stubborn little chin. "Fine. Stay here. Get eaten. I don't care. Honestly, having Lissa of Greentree mysteriously disappear does solve at least one of the problems in my life."

Tomkin thrust himself up, away from the wall, intending to stomp away from her and her irrational stubbornness.

Instead, as he stood the world slid sharply to the left, the fire flashed bright, and the floor buckled.

Then Mags was under his arm again, pushing him upright. "That was stupid."

"Shut up." He wanted to shove off her in disgust, but her shoulder was the only part of the world that wasn't moving.

"Sit back down," she snapped. "You're in no condition to go anywhere."

"I'm getting out of here," Tomkin said. "Before your dragon friend kills me."

Mags sighed. "How?"

"Down the stairs in the courtyard—"

"In the bailey."

"Whatever. Down the stairs to the great hall. There must be other rooms down there along the back of the castle. The cliff path goes that direction, so there must be a back door."

"What are you going to do, just tiptoe past Vorath holding your breath? Didn't you try to sneak up on him once already?"

"This is different." Tomkin pushed away from her and stood on his own. The room only twisted a little before settling down. He took a deep breath of the cool night air. Besides the fact that the light from the fire kept stabbing into his brain, he felt alright. "I don't have a lot of time. Either come with me or sit down and leave me alone." He took one step forward and stopped at the wave of dizziness washing over him. He focused at the doorway across the tower, waiting for it to stop shifting.

Mags huffed in exasperation. "Fine. I'll help you so you don't kill yourself just walking across the bailey. But I refuse to be a part of this. If you want to irritate the dragon, that's up to you. I'd rather stay on his good side." She stepped up next to him and slid under his arm again.

She felt very solid there. Small, but solid. The rest of the room was still slightly off, but he concentrated on the feel of her shoulders beneath his arm and things began to steady. Tomkin grunted and they started forward.

The whole process was a series of little jolts and tugs, with Mags shoving at him and the castle stretching and shifting so his feet kept hitting the ground at unexpected times. The first time his step landed with a stomp, Mags let out a giggle. Two steps later the ground rushed up to meet him again and Tomkin's foot hit with a jarring thud. Mags' shoulders began to shake. He looked at her to see her lips pressed together, trying to keep from laughing out loud.

"What?" he demanded.

The laugh burst out of her. "I thought we were trying to sneak around. You're stomping like an ogre!"

"I can't help it," he said, just as his other foot slammed down onto a stone that had seemed much farther away.

Peels of her laughter echoed off the tower walls. Tomkin growled slightly, but didn't dare shift his arm off her shoulder.

When they stepped out into the rain, it had lightened to a drizzle. The cold water cleared his mind a little bit. Together they stumbled their way out of the tower, into the bailey and to the stairs leading below.

Once there had been a building set over the stairs, but now there was just an open hole in the ground surrounded by rubble. The steps dropped into the interior of the castle.

"I'll have to get Wink to fix this," Mags said, peering at the crumbled base of a wall near the stairs.

"Shh!" Tomkin hissed at her. The noise cut through the rain and he cringed.

"Sorry," she whispered.

He tugged on her shoulder and they continued. The castle had almost stopped moving until Tomkin took his first step and landed too hard on the top stair. It was as though he jarred the castle awake again and it was trying to dislodge him. He stood, clinging to Mags' shoulder, waiting for the motion to stop.

"You should really be sitting down somewhere," Mags pointed out, but at least this time she said it quietly.

"I'll sit when I'm safely away from here." He did his best to let his irritation show in his whisper. "Let's go."

They crept down the stairs, slowly at first, then quicker once there was a wall next to him to steady himself on. The stairs turned to the left and the two of them descended until they stood at the end of the great hall. It was warmer down here, out of the wind and rain.

When Tomkin had crept in the window at the far end earlier, the sunlight had illuminated the dragon and the room. Now everything was black. The windows were three open maws of almost-dark past the long room of blackness. The base of the windows was jagged and Tomkin paused, trying to figure out why. When he had climbed through the one on the right earlier it had been a wide, smooth windowsill.

Then the jaggedness shifted. It was Vorath, laid out along the end of the room, the spikes along his back silhouetted in the windows. With one single flash of lightning, the room burst into light. When the darkness returned the image stayed seared into his mind. Vorath, a dull orange, lay coiled along the end of the great room, his body stretching across all three wide windows with his head and tail circling around in front.

Another glint of orange flashed from the floor near his tail.

"The garnet!" Tomkin whispered. It would be so much better to leave here with the stone. And the sword, of course.

"You're not going over there, are you?" Mags whispered.

"It's on the floor near his tail," Tomkin pulled her forward. "Can you see the sword?" He led her toward Vorath's tail, searching for the little bit of orange he had seen.

They crept forward, the shushing of the rain helping to cover the noise. They reached about where he had seen the garnet flash and Tomkin slid gingerly to his knees, then slid his hands along the floor, searching for the stone.

He felt nothing.

Another flash of lightning showed it just off to his side, bigger and brighter than he expected. He groped through the blackness until he found it.

Except whatever it was he had found was not the garnet. Instead it was flat, like an oversized, irregular coin. Fan-shaped with very small, very tightly packed ridges, it reminded him of a seashell—

—or a scale.

It hadn't been the garnet he'd seen skitter across the dragon's back when his sword had fallen. Scalebreaker had *knocked off one of Vorath's scales*!

Vorath had a weakness.

Tomkin grabbed for Mags' arm and yanked her close to him. Putting his mouth right next to her ear he whispered, "I'm holding one of Vorath's scales!"

"Then where is your stupid garnet?" she demanded, although quietly.

"Must still be in the sword. Do you see it anywhere?"

Beside him, Mags began to run her hands over the floor again. "I wish the lightning hadn't stopped," she whispered.

As if on command, there was a short burst of lightning, yanking Tomkin's attention to the window. It was followed by a long stutter of white light, exposing two things that froze Tomkin's heart.

The first was that Mags' hand was a finger's breadth from the sharp edge of the sword.

The second was, immediately past the sword, chin resting on the floor and yellow eyes fixed on them in his dead, reptilian way, Vorath was awake.

CHAPTER FIFTEEN

UTTER DARKNESS CRASHED BACK into the room accompanied by earth-shaking thunder. Mags shrieked and Tomkin's heart slammed against his chest, and he shoved himself back. Mags grabbed on to his arm and he crouched against her, his eyes stretched wide against the darkness.

The black shape of Vorath's head moved against the window as he lifted it off the floor and hung it over them. Dry air washed across Tomkin's face, the smell searing his nose and throat, tasting like hot metal. Or blood.

A blast of fire shot out of Vorath toward the side of the room. The brightness drove knives of pain into Tomkin's eyes and he buried his face in Mags' shoulder. She cried out and clung to him, shaking.

When the sound of the flames stopped, he looked up cautiously. A broken table near the wall was burning, the flames looking cheerfully out of place in the room.

"We didn't mean to wake you." Mags' voice was thin and trembly. "We're terribly sorry."

In the firelight, the dragon was breathtaking. As he breathed, ripples of ember and darkness shifted across his body, like a living bed of coals.

Is this the sword you are looking for? Vorath slid Tomkin's sword toward them with one long claw, scraping it across the flagstones with a screech.

The hilt of the sword spun toward Tomkin and the garnet flashed in the hilt, as though it held a sliver of the dragon.

Tomkin's heart gave a little lurch to see the sword in one piece. His hands clenched and the scale he had found earlier dug into his palm. When he glanced down at it, the glowing scale peeked out through his fingers, shifting between orange and red in the firelight.

A scale—Vorath was missing a scale.

He ran his gaze along the creature's back, looking for the weak spot. Tomkin glanced at the dragon's face again, trying to gauge emotion on the still, scaled face. The dragon merely looked back at him.

"May I have my sword?" he asked, his voice high and pitiful.

The dragon inclined his head in a nod.

It lay out of reach of where Tomkin knelt. Something in him rebelled at the idea of crawling forward to get it so, slowly, he stood up.

The room shifted and the dragon's head moved without moving. Mags reached for him but he waved her hand away. He could take a couple of steps on his own.

Hopefully.

He pulled himself up straight and took one step forward, then another, keeping his chin raised and his eyes on the dragon. It took three steps through the shifting room before he reached the sword. Carefully, slowly, he squatted and picked it up. The hilt was cold and lifeless beneath his fingers. The sword was heavier than he'd expected. It felt like trying to lift an anvil. There was no way he was going be able to stand up holding it.

He stuck the tip into a crack in the floor, and using the sword as a crutch, pushed himself up. The blade made a grinding noise against the stone and Tomkin had a brief image of himself working for days to hone the blade while his father, brother, and even Granduncle Horace, back from the dead, watched with glares of disapproval.

Tomkin shook off the vision. He was about to redeem himself, about to impress even Horace. Clenching the scale in one hand and leaning on the sword with the other, Tomkin searched again along the dragon's body, looking for the weakness left by the missing scale. The only question would be whether he could reach the area and plunge in the sword before the monster killed him.

He's missing a scale. Tomkin clung to the idea. He's missing a scale.

I am missing many scales. Which one are you referring to?

Tomkin froze.

Let me show you what it is like when a dragon is missing a scale. Vorath sounded bored. He rolled over onto his side, revealing more stomach. *Come see my great weakness.*

Vorath left his clawed hand resting on the floor in front of Tomkin, but as the firelight shimmered across the dragon's side, Tomkin saw a flaw. Right behind the dragon's right arm, in an area where, Tomkin assumed, a sword could pierce the creature and drive straight into his heart.

Tomkin walked forward slowly, planting the sword tip into cracks between stones before each step and leaning on it for balance.

There was something there, a darker spot that didn't reflect the firelight quite right. Tomkin kept waiting for Vorath to make him put down the sword, but the dragon looked unconcerned. Tomkin's grip on the hilt was sweaty. He reached the creature's belly and felt the heat rolling off it as though he stood near a fire.

Tomkin's heart sank. There was the missing scale, the break in the pattern of scales. Tomkin held up the scale in his hand and it fit. But when he pulled it away, it showed the truth no old stories mentioned.

Dragon scales overlap. Each scale layered over the one next to it so there were at least two scales coving every bit of the dragon's skin. Even with this one broken off, Tomkin could only see the slimmest crescent of pale skin. He let the scale drop back down by his side.

Vorath was missing a scale. And it didn't matter.

Tomkin stumbled away from the dragon. There was no way to defeat him. Tomkin was trapped here by a creature whose weakest point still outmatched him, and who planned on killing him in a few hours. It felt as though Vorath had already pulled Tomkin's heart out with one, vicious claw.

Now that you see you cannot kill me, I would like your attention. Vorath rolled onto his stomach and fixed Tomkin with his usual flat gaze. *It is my desire to live here in peace.*

The idea was so ludicrous that a laugh burst out of Tomkin. "Right," he said weakly. "Because no one will mind that a dragon's moved in down the way. You've only been here a few days and people are already terrorized. And you're already stealing livestock."

I must eat. I cannot help it if the sight of me terrorizes the faint-hearted. I won't promise not to prey on the weak, superstitious farmers. But I intend to harm no city or large homestead. I will not attack the men-at-arms. Marshwell is welcome to go about its business free from my interference.

"Except for fainthearted farmers." Tomkin felt his fury begin to rise again at the arrogance of the monster.

Vorath inclined his head slightly. *To impress upon Marshwell how serious I am, I wish them to know I have the duke's son as my prisoner. If the fighting men of Marshwell attack, I will kill you.*

Amidst the vision Tomkin was having of Vorath terrorizing the countryside, Tomkin felt a quiver of hope in his chest. Vorath wasn't planning to kill him in the morning. Maybe there was still a way out.

"You could write a treaty," Mags offered. "Marshwell is an honorable dukedom. They will abide by a treaty."

Vorath nodded his head slowly. *You will write one for me that I will deliver.*

Tomkin's heart faltered at the idea of Vorath flying over Marshwell Holding, circling in the sky, the people below terrified. He imagined the holding burning and his mother, alone, holding a treaty she must sign to save her son.

That was not a story Tomkin could let play out.

"If you show up at the holding," Tomkin said, "the men will rally to fight you, no matter what the treaty says. They'll be too frightened to do anything else." He glanced at Mags, his mind lighting up at an idea. "But you could send her, instead."

Mags' eyebrows rose.

The girl has value to me. But your idea has merit. Humans are stupid when frightened. The dragon considered the two of them. *Write the treaty and send the kobold. He can travel more quickly than a human, correct?*

"Only over short distances," Mags said. "Not all the way to Marshwell."

Then he can walk. Is he near you right now?

Mags nodded uncertainly. "He's always near me."

Have your kobold fetch some paper so we can proceed.

Mags scowled, but raised her voice and said, "Go ahead, Wink."

The room was silent for a few breaths before Wink appeared with paper, the reed pen and a clay bowl that held crushed berries for ink.

"This is a bad idea, mistress. I should not go so far from you. I will not be able to hear you call—" He shot a withering look at the dragon. "—should you need me."

Tomkin couldn't help but agree with Wink. This felt like a terrible idea.

"Just for this one trip." Mags took the paper and set her hand on Wink's shoulder.

She sat on the floor and began to write. Vorath dictated the terms, insisting Marshwell agree to never attack Colbreth Castle. Mags offered suggestions, correcting Vorath if she thought he had misspoken.

"That treaty's very light on Vorath's responsibilities," Tomkin broke in. "*Will not attack a homestead* is vague. What qualifies as a homestead? Multiple buildings? A certain number of people?"

Mags' brow knit slightly. "That is a valid point, Vorath."

"The treaty must state that you will leave every single person in Marshwell alone," Tomkin said, glaring at the dragon, "or no one will sign it. And you must leave our livestock alone. And our buildings. And no flying around terrorizing people."

"You're being awfully restrictive," Mags pointed out.

Tomkin spun around to face her. "Stop siding with him! He should not get *anything*! He has invaded Marshwell, stolen people's livestock and intends to keep—"

Silence! Vorath's voice flooded into Tomkin's mind.

Tomkin flinched back and clapped his hands over his ears. Which didn't stop him from hearing the dragon's next thoughts.

The terms are not up for discussion. Finish and send the kobold. Before I lose patience.

Mags turned back to the paper.

Wink stepped up next to Tomkin, the kobold's enormous eyes peering at the scale in Tomkin's hand. Tomkin handed it to the kobold and the little creature turned it over in his hand. Then he brought the scale to his mouth and stuck out his tongue.

"Don't lick it!" Tomkin hissed, but it was too late.

"This has a surprising amount of iron in it," Wink said,

ignoring Tomkin's grimace. "No wonder dragon scales are so strong."

"Iron? Then how can they grow?"

Wink rolled his eyes. "You have iron in you as well. Many living things do. Although not usually this much." He handed the scale back to Tomkin.

Mags rolled up the treaty and gave it to Wink. "Tomkin, where should Wink go?"

Tomkin looked at Mags and Wink standing next to each other, then turned to Vorath. "It would be better if you sent both of them. There'd be more of a chance of the message getting through if they both—"

Only the kobold. There was a growl deep in Vorath's chest.

Tomkin scowled, but turned to Wink. "How far can you travel when you turn invisible?"

"It's called blinking," Wink said, managing, even from near Tomkin's waist, to look down his long nose at him, "and I can only move a short distance in a blink. But I can't do it too often, it's more tiring to blink than to walk."

Time is of the essence, Vorath said.

Tomkin resisted the urge to scowl at the dragon. "If you can get to the top of the cliffs, head west," Tomkin told Wink. "You should find the King's Highway. It's never far from the river. Take it north and it will lead you to Marshwell Holding. You should reach it an hour or two past dawn."

Go. Before I tire of waiting.

Wink glared at the dragon, then gave Mags a quick bow. He walked to the back of the room and scrambled up to a thin window looking out the back of the castle. He turned to give Mags one last glance, and the dragon one last glare, then he blinked and was gone.

Tomkin stared at the empty window, feeling as though the castle had just closed in on him a bit more. Mags looked at the window as well, chewing her lip.

Wink was gone. All that left was him and Mags. No

warriors, no magic, no power. With the departure of the unpleasant little creature, Tomkin's mind began to churn with the possibilities that had just blinked out the window.

His stomach dropped like a rock over a cliff. Wink could have made them a way out. Or built a cage for the dragon. Or made Tomkin's sword unbreakable. At the very least he could have built a ladder to get them over the walls.

Dread sat in Tomkin's gut like a stone. He turned to face the dragon. "That was what you wanted, wasn't it?"

Vorath merely looked at him. The truth was so obvious. The treaty had been a trick. That whole scene had been a ruse.

"You wanted Wink gone." Tomkin felt sick.

"What are you talking about?" Mags asked.

Vorath settled his chin on the floor. His eye were flat and emotionless, but something about him, the tilt of his head, the smallest curve of his mouth, looked smug.

Tomkin's feet felt as though they had fused to the floor. He forced the question out, even though he could manage nothing over a whisper. "What do you intend to do?"

Vorath looked lazily at Tomkin.

In the morning, before the kobold delivers his message, I will take your body to Marshwell Holding and drop it at the gates. Then I will burn your home to the ground and kill anyone I find.

Everything stopped. Tomkin's breath, his heart, his thoughts. The little hope he'd been holding on to slipped away.

I will raze Marshwell to the ground, and then I will be left in peace. Vorath's eyes slid shut.

Mags gasped. "You lied!" She stepped toward Vorath with her hands clenched into fists at her sides. "You're going to kill them all—including Wink! You sent him to his death!"

The kobold will be spared. Vorath cracked one eye at her. *But you had better hope he is as loyal as you think, Lady Lissa of Greentree.*

Mags shrank back. "You know who I am?"

The boy is not the only one who shouts his thoughts. Vorath turned his head and settled it on the floor next to his tail. His yellow eyes closed.

If your kobold does not return to fix my castle, I will have no more use for you. Except as an example. A sort of purr rumbled deep within his chest. *Not that I will mind. Nothing gets people's attention quite so much as the death of a maiden.*

Mags' face drained of color.

Meanwhile, you may continue your exploration of the castle. The way you were heading leads to the kitchen and storeroom. But temper your hopes. You will find no escape from this place.

CHAPTER SIXTEEN

THERE WAS NO WAY OUT.

Tomkin felt his legs weaken with the truth of it. He wanted to run, to slam into the walls of the castle, to pound until the stones gave way and he could escape. Except he could barely stand. And maybe that's what he'd been doing this whole time, pounding on solid rock with nothing but his fists and expecting the wall to notice.

The little strength left in his body drained out. The first time he'd seen Vorath, he'd known he wasn't brave. Now he knew it didn't matter. Bravery was useless to the powerless.

Tomkin wasn't a hero, he wasn't important, he was just helpless, and more afraid than he'd imagined possible. All the things Tomkin had imagined about himself blew away like smoke.

In their place, fury grew. This whole situation was unbelievable. Why would a dragon, especially one as cunning as Vorath, come to Marshwell? Why spend his time destroying one of Queensland's least important holdings?

"Why are you here?" Tomkin demanded. "Why Marshwell? What do you want?"

The dragon's eyes opened and he fixed Tomkin with a

simmering glare. His voice pounded into Tomkin's mind. *What do I want?* His reptilian head slid forward until Tomkin could have reached out and touched the smooth, layered scales shielding Vorath's face. Tomkin forced himself not to step back. The dragon dropped its voice to an echoing hiss. *What do I want?*

An image slammed into Tomkin's mind. The sword, Granduncle Horace's sword, flashing though the air, glinting in the firelight. And there were scales, not orange, but golden as summer honey.

Tomkin was seeing an image of this hall—but bright with fire. Colorful tapestries burned on the walls, furniture lay shattered on the floor. The world was stark, crisp. Every motion in the room played out in vivid detail.

He wasn't looking through human eyes. He could see his own flaming orange scales rippling in the firelight. He was looking through Vorath's eyes.

He hunched in a corner, encased in darkness, watching the golden dragon spin and slash and burn men around her. Her wings filled the room. She was glorious and powerful and vicious. A goddess compared to the creatures attacking her. She was—

—his mother.

The men had invaded, with their swords and their armor. Their presence defiled this haven, this home, reeking of violence and terror. The place he and his mother would live in, would rule from.

The dragon, flashing yellow and gold in the firelight, screamed and spun, sending the nearest knight's broken body into a corner. Vorath felt a stab of terror as the men closed in on her. Behind her, a man crept along a ledge, holding the sword in front of him.

The four men who still stood attacked her, keeping her attention on them.

The golden dragon stretched out one enormous wing and behind it, a white pucker of flesh was visible, scarred and scaleless. The man on the ledge stared at it and poised himself to jump.

Vorath set one small foot towards her. It glinted orange in the firelight.

"Keep in the shadows!" her voice snapped like a whip in his mind and he flinched back into the darkness.

In that moment, the man on the ledge jumped.

A terrible, reptilian scream ripped out of Vorath's throat. The men spun towards him, the whites of their eyes and the smell of their fear growing as he stepped out of the shadows. The golden dragon twisted toward him, fear for him in her eyes.

Time slowed as the man fell, as he slammed into her side, as he dug the hateful sword deep into her white flesh.

The golden dragon screamed and thrashed, sending the man crashing against the wall. His sword clanged to the stone floor, covered in blood so dark it looked black. An orange gem flickered in its hilt.

The other men backed away from the wounded creature, holding their swords ready.

The golden dragon called to Vorath in his mind, calling him to follow as she staggered through the window and plummeted out of the castle. Vorath slid forward, his head as tall as a man's waist. He hissed, and shot a small stream of fire at the knight. The men spread out around him, holding their swords warily. He wanted to rend them, destroy them with fang and claw and fury.

Around him the beams crossing the ceiling groaned. Fire licked up the walls. A stone above a burning tapestry cracked in the heat.

His mother's call, weak as it was, pulled at him through the window. He turned, spread his wings, and shot after her, sliding into the cool night air.

Ahead of him, she flew low, laboring over the hills to the east until her wings shuddered and she plummeted into a valley.

Vorath let out another scream, this one torn from deep within himself, so full of fury and loss, it ripped something from his very core.

The memory of the golden dragon sinking into the dark crevice faded.

Tomkin blinked and found himself facing Vorath, the creature's jaws inches from his face.

What do I want? Vorath's voice was deadly quiet. *I want revenge.*

The terror that rose in Tomkin squeezed his heart until he thought it might burst. He fell back a step from Vorath's gaze.

He wasn't just trapped in this castle. Even if he could escape, he was doomed. There was no way to win, no way to play the hero. Vorath wanted him dead—him and everyone he loved. That's all there was. The dragon wanted nothing but destruction.

Tomkin felt the dragon's scale bite into his palm as he squeezed it, unbending. Even one single scale was too strong for him. He took in the enormity of the beast, the expanse of scales glowing like embers in the dying firelight. His own body was so negligible that a flick of the dragon's claw would snuff him out.

Tomkin could do nothing. It would be easier to shove Colbreth Castle off the cliff than to affect the dragon in any way.

He fell back another step and his shoulder bumped into Mags where she stood, shrunk in on herself.

Vorath's breath came out in a furious blast of air. *Get out of my hall.*

Tomkin shoved the scale into his pocket, and using the sword as a crutch, grabbed Mag's hand, pulling her away from the dragon. She turned wide eyes on him, her face mirroring what he felt. He tugged her toward the door leading to rooms along the back wall, where the lake sat against the castle wall.

Tomkin turned his back on the dragon and Mags ducked under his arm. He wasn't sure whether she was offering support or hiding, but he leaned on her, using the solid feel of her to steady himself.

They took a step toward the door, then another. The weight of Vorath's gaze on his back was palpable.

He ducked his head next to Mags' ear. "Are you okay?"

She didn't answer, just walked toward the door with her face set in a determined scowl. But she was pale and her arm, wound around his back, quivered. He squeezed her shoulders, but felt his own arm tremble.

The door to the kitchens sat in the far left corner of the great hall. It took ages to reach it. When they did, Mags reached for the door handle. With a loud creak the door pushed open and they both flinched at the noise. Mags glanced back at Vorath. Tomkin followed her gaze.

The table had burned low, glowing a deep red and leaving most of the room in darkness. The last of the light glinted off Vorath's scales. Ripples of shadowed red flowed across the darkness, turning the dragon into a mountain of living coals. Bright as death.

Out the gaping windows, through what was left of the storm, the hint of a moon rose over the eastern hills.

Mags' body began to shake harder. Tomkin pushed on her shoulder, turning her away from the sight of the dragon and stepping them into the doorway. The light from the great hall illuminated just enough past them to show stairs descending into darkness. Mags held back at the sight.

"C'mon," Tomkin whispered, "we'll find a way out."

Mags let out a burst of breath, a laugh tinged with terror. She reached over and pushed the door shut behind them, dropping everything into blackness.

"No, we won't."

PART III

It didn't matter whether Tomkin was heroic or not.
There was no room for a hero in this story.

-From Keeper Mikal's retelling
of Tomkin and the Dragon

CHAPTER SEVENTEEN

THEY STOOD in the darkness for a moment, not moving. What were they going to do now? Mags was right, they weren't going to find a way out. And even if they did, what would that matter? Even if they could escape, before they could reach Marshwell, it was going to be destroyed.

"Stay here," Mags said, wiggling out from under Tomkin's arm and disappearing into the darkness.

He grabbed for her, but felt nothing but air.

"Where are you going?" He leaned on the sword, hoping he was keeping his balance as well as he thought he was. The beginning of the stairs had been very close. The way his day was going, if he fell down the stairs, he'd probably end up impaling himself on the sword.

"To find us some light."

He heard her rustle forward and down.

The darkness of the hall sat there like something dead, or decaying. It wasn't in the smell. The hall smelled of stale spices and dampness. It was in the feel of the air. Or maybe it was in Tomkin's mind. Vorath had allowed them to come here because there was nothing to find. They were just wasting time until morning.

He saw a flash of light illuminate Mags' face. Then another. The third time, the flame stayed lit, tiny and dim. Mags leaned down and blew gently. Within a couple of breaths, Tomkin could see the stairs enough to begin to descend them. On the floor in front of where she knelt was a small wad of fabric burning quickly. Mags tucked a small flint into a pocket of her dress.

Slowly, one hand on the stone wall for balance, Tomkin moved to where she was. The walls and the floor remained reasonably still.

Mags pulled a torch out of a ring on the wall and touched the end to the burning fabric.

"You have flint?" Tomkin asked. "What other useful things do you have?"

She gave him an annoyed look. "You didn't bring flint?"

Tomkin began to shake his head, but the aching made him stop.

She rolled her eyes and slid back under his arm, steadying him. Holding the torch in front of them, she started down the hallway. "Honestly, did you put *any* thought into this plan of yours? Or did you just grab the first impractical weapon you could find and race off unprepared? Did you bring any food? Or water?"

"Yes, I brought food and water," Tomkin snapped. "It was in my boat. Which your dragon friend burned and sank."

"He's not my friend," she said quietly, her shoulders stiffening under his arm.

The torchlight flickered on the walls, causing as much shadow as light.

A twinge of guilt worked its way through Tomkin's irritation. "Sorry."

Silence stretched between them. Tomkin was tired of fighting with her, tired of saying things to make her mad.

"I was serious before," he said, trying to make his voice friendly, "when I said you should go to the Scale Mountains.

There are all sorts of deserted forts and keeps scattered throughout the Scales. No one claims them because none of the duchies over there are wealthy enough to want the expense of keeping them up. You'd be far away from Greentree, and with a little searching you could find a nice one that didn't need too much work. Between you and Wink, you could make something amazing."

Mags gave him a sidelong glance.

"And if you're dead set on living in one with a dragon, you might find one of those, too...."

She jabbed her hip out at him and he stumbled. But she held him up and a smile curled the edges of her mouth. The hallway they were in stretched on, unbroken, until the end where three doors were tucked close together. One straight ahead of them and one on each wall.

Mags slipped out from under Tomkin's arm to open the one on the left, revealing a small, moldy closet. Across the hall, the other door opened into a storeroom that was narrow but long, running to the right for a good way. Tomkin walked over to one of the arrow-slit windows. He climbed onto the box below it, surprised when the world didn't spin at all. Fresh, cool air blew past his face.

Outside the window the rain had stopped and the clouds were sailing past like the tattered remains of a battle flag. Bits of starlight flashed in the gaps. The top of the cliff across from him was lit by moonlight. The sliver of world he could see below the window was pitch-black.

"Give me the torch."

"Don't tell me what to do," she snapped.

Tomkin took a deep breath, then turned around and gave her a deep bow. "May I please have the torch, sweet Mags?"

She narrowed her eyes at him but passed the torch. He turned and held it out the window. Beneath him, about the level of the floor of the storeroom, slivers of torchlight glittered back up at him.

"The lake is right against the castle here." He peered to his right, trying to see where the water ended, but could make out nothing in the darkness.

He turned around to catch Mags shuddering. "What's wrong?"

"I'm not going out on a lake. We need to find a way out that doesn't involve water."

Tomkin bit back the first thing that came to mind to say to her. Then the second.

He forced his voice to be patient. "There *isn't* another way out. From the south wall of the castle there are rotting, broken steps winding down the cliff to a dock on the river. There's no way out of there without a boat, and Vorath sank mine. The east and north walls have sheer drops to the river. This western wall is our only hope. There's not much room between the castle wall and the cliff that rises above us, so the lake can't be very big. And it's only over on this end of the castle.

"From the bailey I saw a flat field behind the wall. There was a path that came from the lake and went all the way up the cliff. If we can get to the top, we're free."

Mags shook her head in a fast, twitchy way. "I'm not going on any water." Her voice sounded brittle. She stood in the flickering torchlight with her arms wrapped around herself tightly.

Tomkin climbed off the box, using the sword as a crutch. He walked up to her and handed her the torch. The fresh air at the window had done wonders for his head and the world felt stable. He put his arm around her shoulder anyway and steered her back out of the room. "Let's not worry about how we're going to escape until we find out if it's even possible."

"It's not," Mags said. "Vorath wouldn't have let us down here if it was."

Tomkin's heart dropped a little at her words. He'd been

pushing that thought away from his mind. "Maybe Vorath doesn't know what's here. How could he? He's too big to fit."

"I'm pretty sure he's looked at the western wall to see if there's a door back there," Mags said. She pushed his arm off her shoulder and cracked open the last door.

A hissing noise slipped out. She froze and looked at Tomkin with wide eyes. When the noise didn't change, she pulled the door open the rest of the way. The sound grew richer and deeper, a sort of loud shushing.

"What is that?" she asked.

Tomkin shook his head. Whatever it was, it sounded far away.

Their torchlight illuminated the near end of a kitchen. It felt chilly and cavernous, and it smelled damp.

A long, sagging table ran down the middle of the room. Counters, shelves, and more counters, lined both walls. The right-hand wall of the kitchen was broken by another arrow-slit window and the gaping mouth of an oven.

Tomkin's bare arm felt chilled. The room was humid, cold, and cave-like. He could smell the damp, plant smell of the lake and their footsteps echoed hollowly. Next to the door were shelves holding moldy towels, a stack of metal bowls, and a pile of torches. Mags gave a little hoot and grabbed a torch.

She lit it and handed it to Tomkin. He started down one side of the room while Mags walked down the other. The kitchen was a mess. No one must have been here since the night Granduncle Horace had chased away that dragon— Vorath's mother.

No wonder Vorath wanted this place. Horace hadn't known he'd killed the beast. Everyone thought he'd just wounded it and driven it off. His ballads would grow after Tomkin got back and told the whole story.

If Tomkin got back.

He felt a cold breeze from deeper in the room. The

shushing noise came from that direction, so Tomkin held his torch high and walked closer. On the other side of the saggy table, Mags stayed with him.

His torchlight had just reached the back wall when Mags gave a little shriek and stumbled back. The floor ahead of Tomkin glittered. He stepped closer.

It was water.

Cut into the floor against the back wall of the kitchen was a channel, wider than Tomkin was tall. Black water rushed out from a tunnel on his right, and into darkness to his left. It was water from the lake, diverted through the castle, and it was the roar of the waterfall outside they'd been hearing.

It was brilliant, really, to have the fresh lake water run through the kitchen. If he'd thought about it, he would already have known it happened. After all, from the river below he'd seen a waterfall land behind the castle, and another flow out of a small arch in the front. There hadn't been this much water, though. The little channel must be swollen from the storm.

The remains of a wooden fence ran along the channel, but it had rotted long ago and now hung on one good post. Tomkin walked to the edge of the water, ignoring Mags' whimper, and peered upstream through the short tunnel, which must lead to the lake. At the far end of the tunnel, the torchlight glinted off rusted metal bars.

"I need more light!" he said to Mags.

She nodded, her eyes wide and fixed on the water. She backed away a few steps, before turning to run back for more torches. She returned, along the same side of the room as Tomkin, clutching as many torches as she could hold. They stuck them in pitchers, vases, sconces, anything they could find to hold them.

With all the torches lit, the surface of the water glimmered as it rushed past, throwing golden reflections on the ceilings and walls. Like the room had filled with golden fairies, flittering about too quickly to see.

He turned to say as much to Mags, but she had retreated from the water and sank into a ball, hugging her knees and staring at the water.

Tomkin put his sword on the table and grabbed a long, wooden pole leaning against the end of the cabinets. There was an iron ring fixed to the wall where the tunnel began. Tomkin gave it an experimental tug, and it held firm. Holding the ring in one hand and the pole in the other, he leaned out over the channel and reached the pole upstream toward the grate.

He did his best to ignore the whimpering sound from Mags.

The pole was unwieldy, but Tomkin managed to bang it against the grate, resulting in a dull but solid-sounding noise. His heart sank. The rust hadn't compromised the grate enough to damage it. It was still unyielding metal.

The end of the pole dipped into the water and wrenched against his grip. Tomkin fought to lift it back out, but the water slammed the end of the pole into the far wall and ripped it out of his hand. In a breath, it rushed down the channel and disappeared into the darkness.

Tomkin held his torch out over the water and looked downstream. No metal grate sat at that end, just a gaping hole. Tomkin's hand tightened on the ring. Anything that fell in this water would be swept out the front of the castle and fall onto the rocks along the river a hundred feet below.

CHAPTER EIGHTEEN

TOMKIN STOOD at the corner of the wall and looked down the tunnel toward the lake. Along the edge of the water, a metal rod was attached to the stone wall like a railing. Holding the iron ring again, he leaned out over the water.

"Will you *please* stop doing that!" Mags hissed.

Tomkin ignored her and held his torch as far into the tunnel as he could. Halfway down, the railing turned and disappeared into a dark recess. Past that, the tunnel continued, with the railing, all the way to the metal grate. He pulled himself back into the kitchen. Mags gripped the table with white knuckles.

Tomkin gave her a little smile and patted the kitchen wall. "There's a room along the channel, right behind this wall."

Three cabinets back from the channel he found a large door he had taken for a pantry. When he pulled it open, his torch lit up a little stone alcove off the channel, full of gently swirling water. He was standing on a little stone dock. In front of him, two steps led down to the water.

And floating in the water was a little boat.

"Mags!" he called to her, trying to keep his voice low enough that the rushing noise of the water would mask it if the dragon were listening. "This must have been how they brought supplies into the kitchen!" He moved down the steps. The little boat filled almost the entire surface of the water.

"It's clever, don't you think?" He glanced back over his shoulder and saw just the top of Mags' head sticking around the corner.

"Oh stop it," he said. "This water is barely moving. Come in here."

Mags stepped around the corner, and stepped down one step, leaning close to the wall. She shook her head.

Tomkin almost snapped at her, until he noticed her torch wavering in her shaking hand. "Okay," he said, trying to make his voice kinder. "If you're not going to come all the way in, will you please grab a couple more torches? There are sconces in here and it would be nice to see better."

She nodded and hurried back out. Tomkin's torchlight filtered to the flagstone bottom of the alcove. The water wasn't deep here, maybe only up to his waist. The boat was small but deep, with its sides coming up well above the water line. It was tied to a peg on the wall.

The metal railing Tomkin had seen from the kitchen ran into this room, anchored to the wall above the waterline, and then ran back out along the channel toward the metal grate. He pulled on the railing to see if the years had weakened it, but it was firmly attached.

Mags came back and set a small oil lamp on the kitchen table past the door. She brought in three torches and placed them into sconces on the wall, filling the room with light. Tomkin thanked her, and she nodded before going back to stand near the door. He gave the boat a little shove. It dipped and clunked into the far wall before bobbing back into place. Gingerly, he stepped into it.

Mags gasped as the little boat sank deeper into the water. It wobbled a bit under his feet, but held.

Tomkin lowered himself onto the seat, causing the boat to rock slightly. Water seeped in through a crack in the left side of the hull. When he leaned over to the right to lift the crack above the waterline, water rushed in from that side as well. Tomkin sat still and tall, but the water pooled deeper and deeper in the boat, seeping in from unseen holes, swirly cold around his feet.

"Get out, get out, get out," Mags pleaded quietly.

He shook his head. "The water's shallow. If the boat sinks, I'll just climb out."

She clamped her mouth shut, but he could still hear her humming something between a chant and a whimper.

Tomkin leaned forward, trying to figure out where the water was coming from. He pushed on a piece of wood at the bottom of the boat. His finger pushed straight through, like pressing through damp paper.

A gush of water rushed in. Tomkin yanked his hand back and Mags made a squeaking, strangling noise.

Tomkin clambered out of the sinking boat, and cold water swirled and splashed up to his knees before he got his foot on the step and sloshed his way up to Mags.

The boat listed toward them, farther and farther until the rim of it dipped below the waterline, then water swirled in and it sank to the bottom in a breath.

Tomkin's heart sank with it.

Underwater, the boat wavered in the torchlight.

"Well," Mags said brightly, "looks like we need to find a different way out!"

Tomkin spun around to face her. "There *is* no other way out!" He flung his arm at the channel. "This tunnel is the way *out*. The *only* way out."

Mags scowled at him. "You think our way out is up a channel flowing too fast for us to swim? And then through a thick metal grate?" She stepped away from the wall enough to get right in his face. "Have you forgotten that big stick you dropped? Anything in that water will be ripped downstream and fall a hundred feet to be crushed on the rocks below." She tossed a scornful look at the water. "It was a stupid plan even before you sank the boat."

Fury rose inside him like a physical burning wave. "You're right, Mags, every single thing that touches this channel is going to be killed instantly." He stomped back down the steps into the water.

Out of the corner of his eye he saw Mags reach for him, her eyes wide and her face draining of color. He waded in to his waist, grabbed at the rope securing the boat, and yanked at the knot, trying to untie it. The rope was rough and sharp hairs kept stabbing into his fingers, but he wanted to fight against it, to make *something* bend to his will. Even if it was only a stupid rope. With a final tug it untied. He turned and gave the broken, useless boat a shove.

It moved slowly underwater toward the channel, until the current wrenched the front edge into the tunnel and out of sight.

Tomkin turned to find Mags shrunk back against the wall, staring terrified at the empty water.

"Go back to your crumbling tower." Tomkin splashed his way back to the stairs and up into the kitchen. "You're not the one scheduled to be killed in a few hours. You can continue in naive bliss until Vorath eats you. And I can search for a way out in peace."

He stormed over to the edge of the channel again, grabbing the iron ring and leaning over the water to see the grate.

"Stop doing that!" Mags commanded.

Tomkin ignored her. The top of the grate disappeared up into the rocks. If people had ever used that boat to bring supplies into the kitchen, there must be a way to lift the grate. He pulled himself back into the kitchen. On the wall next to the boat room door sat a square cabinet door. Tomkin pulled it open.

Inside was a large, wooden wheel with long, smoothed posts sticking out of it, like the steering wheel of a ship. Iron chain glinted from behind it. Part of the chain snaked up into a hole above the wheel, disappearing into the wall.

It was a winch.

Tomkin put his torch in a sconce next to the door and grabbed one of the spokes. Bracing himself, he pulled on the spoke.

The wheel groaned, the chain clinked, but nothing moved.

He adjusted his grip and tried again.

Nothing happened.

"You might want to move the locking pin." Mags pointed at a spike of wood set through a hole in the wheel. She reached past him and pulled it out, flourishing the long, thin piece of wood at him.

Tomkin shot a glare at her that he hoped she could feel. "I would have seen it." He pulled again and this time the wheel turned slowly, the iron chain shifting and snapping taunt.

The wheel felt as though it were mired in a pit of sludge, but it moved. Slowly. Besides the small clinking of the chain, it moved quietly. He grabbed the next spoke and pulled until he had turned the wheel one full turn.

"Go see if it's moving," he grunted, reaching for the next spoke.

Mags' eyes grew wide and she shook her head nervously.

The muscles in his arms were aching with the effort of pulling the wheel. "Just go stick your head around the corner and look!"

She backed away from him, pale and shaking.

"Brave enough to domesticate a dragon, but terrified of a little water." He glared at her. "Put the locking pin in."

Mags shoved the pin back in. Gently, Tomkin let up on the wheel. It groaned, but the pin held.

Snatching the torch out of Mags' hand, Tomkin stomped to the channel. "I'm going to make you turn the wheel next time!" He grabbed the ring and leaned out over the water again.

The lowest bar on the grate was covered in dripping moss. Finally, something was working. He felt a twinge of despair when he saw how much more he needed to lift the grate, but he pushed that thought out of his mind. He pulled himself back into the kitchen and took a moment to think through his situation. There was a way out, if they could find a boat.

Tomkin walked back over to Mags. "C'mon. I need to talk to the brave dragon-charmer girl. I assume she's hidden inside there somewhere." He led her back away from the water. When they reached the far end of the kitchen he took her shoulders in his hands and looked into her face.

"I need your help. If you stay this far from the water, can you calm down enough to help me?"

Mags' eyes flicked over his shoulder toward the channel, then back to his face. She nodded tersely.

"Good." Tomkin patted her shoulder and walked over to the nearest cabinet, opening it to look inside. "We need to find something that floats."

There was no sound from Mags behind him. He glanced at her. She was standing with her arms crossed, shaking her head.

"Look, Mags, I don't want to drown in the channel and be tossed over the waterfall either." Mags' eyes widened and a whimper escaped her. That might not have been the best thing to say. "But we either spend a couple minutes on the water pulling ourselves out of this place, or we're killed by a dragon."

Mags still said nothing.

"Killed by a dragon!" he shouted.

"Shh!" She glanced at the kitchen door.

Tomkin gritted his teeth, but forced his next words out quietly. "No one intelligent would think this was a hard choice."

At his tone, her eyebrows shot down into a scowl and she dropped her arms to her side.

He took a deep breath and tried to make the next words come out calm and reassuring. "I will keep you safe on the water, Mags. We just need to get out of here before Vorath kills us." He looked at her, hoping she'd hear what he was saying. "Or, at least, kills me."

Mags kept scowling, but nodded.

"Great." Tomkin turned away from her. "Let's see what we can find that floats. A cabinet door?" Tomkin walked over to the biggest cabinet door. He could pull it off, but it wasn't going to float very well in the surging water of the tunnel.

"Will that huge copper cauldron work?" Mags asked.

Tomkin turned to find Mags looking in the gaping oven. A deep, copper pot, big enough to stew an entire pig in, sat against one wall.

"That's perfect!" Tomkin slapped her on the shoulder enthusiastically, ignoring the sick expression on her face.

"Won't it be too heavy to float?"

"Not if it's wide enough," Tomkin said, reaching into the oven and pulling it out. The surface of the pot was covered in a green and brown patina. He knocked on it with his fingers and it rang dully. "Elton and I took all the pots from the kitchen one summer and organized pot races with the other kids on the fish pond. We forgot to bring them back inside when we were done." Tomkin laughed. "The cook thought she'd been robbed and raised such a commotion." Tomkin glanced at Mags. She was staring at him, pale faced. "Anyway, some pots sank, but some floated quite well. It's not about the weight, it all depends on the shape. We didn't float any this large, but it looks good. The base is thick and heavy, which will keep it from tipping. The sides are tall, to keep water from sloshing in, and they're thin, to keep it from being too heavy. I think it's going to work great."

"We can't both fit," Mags said.

Tomkin nodded. "We'll have to go one at a time. See if you can kneel in it."

Mags glared at him, but threw one leg into the pot, then the other, shimmying down until she knelt on the bottom. The edges of the pot came up to her armpits.

"Excellent!" Tomkin walked around the pot, finding two large handles on the sides. "We'll tie a rope around this handle and I'll keep ahold of that. Then you can climb in the pot and pull yourself out of the tunnel along the railing that runs along the wall. When you get past the grate and around the corner, there's sure to be a place to dock. You can climb out of the pot and just let it go, I'll draw it back to me with the rope, then I'll do the same thing and meet you out there."

Mags just stared at him. "That is the most horrifying plan I've ever heard."

CHAPTER NINETEEN

TOMKIN LIFTED the pot and carried it to the boat room. "Let's see if this floats." Gently, he set it on the water. The pot sank until the base of it sat beneath the waterline, but stayed upright.

"This is a great boat, Mags." Tomkin pulled it back onto the bottom step. "Let's find a rope before we do anything. We don't want to lose this beauty down the channel."

Mags nodded and went back into the kitchen. He felt a pang of pity for her, being so terrified. But he had to admit it was nice to have a break from her scathing tongue.

They did find a cabinet full of coiled ropes, but they were all in various stages of disintegration. Under a sink, though, Tomkin found a long chain attached to an oddly shaped bucket. Instead of being round, it was a long, thin rectangle, no wider than Tomkin's outstretched hand.

"What do you think this is for?" Tomkin held the bucket so Mags could see it.

She cocked her head slightly. "It would fit out the arrow-slit window."

"You're a genius!" Tomkin took the bucket over to the wall to check. Sure enough, the rectangle just fit through the window. When he turned, Mags looked pleased, the expression softening her face. It took Tomkin a moment to realize it was because of what he'd said.

He paused, realizing how few times he'd said anything kind enough to make her happy. Her small smile made the room feel less threatening, and he found himself smiling back. "You should try to look happy more often," he said, climbing off the box and nudging her shoulder with his as he passed her. "It does wonders for your face."

She snorted at him, following him back to the boat room.

The awkward rectangular pot turned out to be perfect. Tomkin was able to thread the chain through the handle of the copper pot all the way to the bucket, which was too large to fit through. He looked around and found a hook on the wall. He yanked and pulled on it with all his might, but it didn't budge. Satisfied that the hook would hold, he hooked several links of the chain onto it. Tomkin picked up the copper pot and set it in the water at the edge of the stairs.

"Okay, the chain's well attached here, and I'm going to keep hold of it too," Tomkin said, turning to Mags. "You'll get in the…" He glanced at the copper pot, which now listed toward the side with the chain knot. "…boat, and grab hold of that railing on the wall.

"You're going to pull yourself along that rail out of this room, around the corner into the channel and out past the grate. I've seen the rail, it goes all the way out. I'll stay right here and hold the chain so that if anything happens, I can pull you back in here."

Mags shrank back a little farther against the wall, tiny and frightened. He set the chain down and went over to her. He set his hand on her shoulder and could feel her quaking.

"It's going to be alright. Let's go raise the grate."

He went to the winch, Mags right on his tail. She pulled out the locking pin and Tomkin strained against the wheel.

The first few turns were easier than last time, but then the winch slowed, forcing Tomkin to fight for every inch.

Mags stepped up to the other side of the wheel and began to push. Tomkin gave her a tight smile and the two of them grunted and shoved. The gears of the winch groaned and the iron chain complained over the use, but the noise was quiet enough to be drowned out by the water. At least Tomkin hoped Vorath couldn't hear. It would be unpleasant to drag themselves outside just to run into the dragon.

Tomkin doggedly kept turning. *This is the way out.* He pulled the wheel an eighth of a turn. Another eighth. *This is the way out.* This was another job that Elton would have handled with ease. Probably with panache. Probably without any of this grunting and wheezing. When he thought he couldn't turn the wheel another hair's breadth, he paused. "Go see if it's high enough."

Mags nodded and gingerly let go of the wheel. She took a few steps and, clinging to the wall, peaked around the corner and up the tunnel. When she turned around her face was lit with that smile again.

"It's almost all the way up! There's plenty of room to fit under it." She pushed the locking pin into place.

Tomkin groaned in relief and released the wheel. The wheel settled back to rest on the pin and the wood crunched. Both of them froze.

The wood shifted slightly, the iron chain groaned up inside the wall, but nothing else happened.

Tomkin sank back against the wall and gave Mags a smile. It felt weak and a little sickly. Heaving himself back up, he led the way back to the boat room.

"Okay, climb in." He grabbed the sides to stabilize it.

When she didn't move he glanced up. She was pressed back in the corner again, her face white, her eyes wide, hands pressed to her mouth.

"Mags," he fought to keep his voice calm, "please come get in the boat."

She shrank back farther.

A wave of exhaustion rolled over Tomkin. Why was she was still fighting him? Since he had met her, she had fought him every step of the way. Now he had a plan. A good plan. A plan that was going to work, and she was still fighting him. If Elton was here she'd be throwing herself into his arms, begging to be rescued.

Tomkin shoved that thought aside. It didn't matter what his brother would do or what should happen if this were the kind of adventure story where the hero returned home to be immortalized.

What mattered was that he and Mags needed to leave. And this was the way out, if Mags could just be brave enough to do it.

Tomkin let go of the cold edge of the copper pot and walked up to Mags. He set his hands on her shoulders and looked into her face. Her eyes flicked to him, then returned to the water.

"Mags?"

Her eyes flicked to him again. He had been shoving aside thoughts of the coming morning this whole time, trying not to think of what awaited him. Now he let the fear of it in through a little crack. "In a few hours the sun will rise, Vorath will take me, kill me, and drop my body at my home, before burning it to the ground." The crack split open into a gaping hole and Tomkin's voice wavered. "We need to get out and at least try to warn someone."

Mags turned her gaze to him and locked on to his face. She was so frightened that Tomkin felt his heart twist in sympathy. "Can we please get out of here?" he asked.

"I can't do it," she whispered.

"Yes, you can."

She shook her head violently.

Tomkin's patience broke with an almost audible sound. He pulled his hands off her shoulders and clenched them into fists at his sides.

"Lissa of Greentree," he snapped, his voice sounding surprisingly like his father's.

Her gaze flashed up to him and her eyes narrowed at his tone.

"You claim," he continued, "to have left home, changed your name, and decided you were the one who would write the story of your life. Yet when it comes time to act, you're cowering in the corner like a frightened child."

Mags pushed herself off the wall, eyes blazing.

"You stood up to Princess Ellona," he continued. He flung his hand in the direction of the great hall. "You stood up for yourself and made a deal with a dragon! It was a stupid deal. But you did it. That level of bravery is...is inhuman."

Her eyes narrowed suspiciously at the combination of insult and compliment.

"You keep telling me you don't need to be rescued. But this is the first time you've acted like you do."

Her jaw dropped in indignation. "I do *not* need the younger son of some lesser duke to rescue me."

"Really? Because you look too terrified to move. Shall I toss you over my shoulder and carry you from the dragon's lair?"

She shot him a look of such venom, he took a half step back.

She stepped forward until she was right in his face. "I don't need *anyone* to rescue me." She spun and marched toward the pot. Hurriedly, as though trying not to think about it, she climbed in.

The pot sank a little more, and Tomkin leaned forward to hold it while she got settled. Her knuckles were white on the edge of the pot as she tucked herself into it. When she was kneeling, she flashed him a defiant look. But the defiance looked brittle. He hoped it would last long enough to get them out.

He gave her a nod. "Alright, She Who Writes Her Own Story, grab that railing over there, and get to it."

"Fine." She reached over to the far wall and grabbed the iron bar. Tugging on it, she pulled the copper pot along the wall toward the channel. When she reached the end of the boat room, the pot bounced in the rougher water. She stayed there for a breath, then glanced over her shoulder.

"You'll hold on to the chain?" Her voice was tight.

Tomkin nodded. "And it's anchored to the wall. Even if you lose your grip, you can't go far, I'll pull you back in here."

Mags clung to the rail for a long minute.

"Mags," Tomkin said. "You are the most determined person I've ever met. And it's just a little farther."

Mags straightened in the copper pot and looked back at the tunnel. She pulled the pot forward, shoving it out into the channel as though daring it to push back.

It did push back, and she let out a small scream. But she held on to the rail, and with a noise somewhere between a shout and a growl dragged the pot upstream, around the corner, and out of sight.

Tomkin stood in the empty boat room, watching the chain drop into the water, trailing after her. He let the cold iron run through his hands in spurts and jolts as Mags tugged herself up the tunnel.

With each link of the chain that slid through his fingers, he felt the terror of the day receding. It was working. She must be near the grate by now, and after that the water would open into the lake. She was almost safe. It would be a matter of moments before the copper pot came floating back for him. Then Tomkin would pull himself out, too. He wouldn't waste time being scared of the water. He'd just get himself out and the two of them could be up the cliff and on their way north.

Another handful of links slid through his fingers.

No. That's not what was going to happen. At the top of the cliff, their paths would part. Mags would head west to the Scale Mountains, and Tomkin north to Marshwell Holding.

It was an uncomfortable thought that she would be going in a different direction. Somehow, in the bits of the future he'd let himself imagine, his mind had offered up the story of her racing back to Marshwell with him, warning everyone of Vorath.

Somehow, when he imagined himself running home alone, her absence was almost palpable.

A deep splintering sound ripped through the silence of the boat room.

Tomkin whirled around, trying to figure out what the noise was. It couldn't be from the copper pot, the noise was too wooden.

There was another crack, this one longer, like the slow splitting of a log, and Tomkin realized it came from behind him.

From the kitchen.

An image of Vorath filled his mind. The scaled head battering through the kitchen door, the great creature slithering into the kitchen, destroying the table, the counters, everything.

It was the third crack that snapped the truth into Tomkin's head.

The winch.

Tomkin dropped the chain, praying the hook would hold if Mags needed it, and took the stairs two at a time. He reached the winch just as a fourth crack caused it to shudder. A gap in the wood spread from the locking pin toward the center of the wheel. Tomkin grabbed at a spoke, trying to shift the weight of the wheel off the pin. His efforts split the crack further.

He grabbed opposite sides of the split at the same time, trying to hold it together.

Tomkin's arms and back strained against the heavy wheel. His ears strained down the tunnel, listening for any sound from Mags. She had to be past the grate by now.

The winch held for a moment, then with a crack like thunder, it broke in half.

Behind the spokes, the coil of chain burst free and spun, length after length of chain flying up into the hole in the wall. Tomkin's breath was ripped away with it.

He grabbed a torch and raced to the edge of the channel. His torchlight glinted off the grate sunk deep in the water.

There was no pot.

"Lissa!" Tomkin hissed into the tunnel, not daring to call louder. The image of Vorath breaking into the kitchen was too fresh in his mind. "Lissa!"

A large shape moved and Tomkin held the torch out farther. Through the grate he caught a flash of copper.

She had made it through. He almost dropped his torch into the water in relief.

With a dull clank, the pot bumped against the grate. Its handle spun past.

"Lissa?" he called, the strange motion of the pot sending a dart of fear into him.

With a lurch, the current caught at the copper pot and slammed it against the grate. It listed sharply away from him and he saw the bottom of the pot for just a moment before it sank beneath the black water.

CHAPTER TWENTY

IN THE SPACE between that heartbeat and the next, Tomkin felt as though he had been pulled under with her—water, chilling and raw, dragging him under, snaking cold, dead fingers around his heart.

"LISSA!" The word tore out of him, but the sound of the water broke it apart, pulling the fragments downstream and tossing them over the waterfall to the river below.

He lunged into the channel, one hand grabbing the metal rail along the wall, his other reaching for the grate but closing on nothing. The gap between him and Mags stretched vast and uncrossable.

The cold water shoved against him with so much force he grabbed the rail with both hands. He tried to pull himself upstream, but the current was too strong. His arms shook, exhausted, and his fingers began to loosen against his will.

"Tomkin!" the voice was thin and barely audible above the sounds of the water, but it came from the kitchen.

Tomkin slid down the rail back to the kitchen floor and scrambled out of the water. He stood up and stopped. The kitchen was empty. "Lissa?"

"Tomkin!"

Tomkin ran toward the window, clambering up on the counter to press his face against the thin arrow slit. Something moved near the bottom of it.

"Tomkin?" Mags whispered, terrified. "Tomkin! The grate closed! I—"

"Are you alright?" Tomkin interrupted.

"Yes. When the grate fell it pinned the chain down, but I was around the corner already and, since I could see the steps out, I just climbed out of the pot and pulled myself along the railing to the end." She sounded proud of herself.

Tomkin sank onto his knees, dropping his forehead forward against the narrow window. "I thought you were—" his voice shook slightly.

Mags' small hand reached in and Tomkin closed it in his own. It was freezing.

"Are you okay?" she asked. "You're shaking. Your face is in the shadows, I can't see you very well. Are you alright?"

He held her small, icy hand in his and began to rub it, trying to put some warmth back into it. "The pot, Mags. It...." His chest tightened at the memory. "I thought you...." The window was wide enough for him to see her face. "I'm so sorry." The words came out in a whisper.

"It's alright. I'm okay." A smile flashed in the darkness and she squeezed his hand. "I did it, you know." The note of pride was back in her voice. "I climbed out of the pot, even though I didn't know how deep the water was, and pulled myself over to the steps."

The solid feeling of her hand began to steady him and Tomkin took a deep breath. "Of course you did. The lake is lucky it didn't try to stop you. Who knows what you'd say to a body of water that vexed you."

Mags let out a little laugh. "What happened with the grate?"

Tomkin glanced back at the winch, hanging broken on the wall. The chain was gone. It must have been dragged up into the wall. The winch was not only broken, it was utterly useless.

"The winch…cracked."

Her breath caught. "How will you get out?"

"I can…put it back together." That wasn't a complete lie. He could piece the winch back together. It wouldn't open the grate again, but… "Mags, start up the cliff. You need to get away from here. Head west to the Scales. Get as far as you can before dawn, then find somewhere to hide. Vorath wants to destroy the holding. If you're not on the road to Marshwell, you should be fine. But be careful."

"I'm not leaving you," she said, indignant.

Tomkin felt his stomach drop a little. The wall between them felt like the wall of a prison cell, stretching around him, unbreakable. He shook his head. "It's stupid for you to wait. We're not going the same direction anyway. You should get started."

"You'll be coming soon?" she asked.

Tomkin squeezed her hand slightly. He forced the words out. "Yeah, I'll be right behind you."

She stood silent for a long moment, her hand small and cold in his. He didn't want to let go of it.

"Lissa," Tomkin said. "I'm glad I met you. And I'm sorry I judged you before I did. I hope you find a good place in the Scales."

"When I do," she asked, her voice trembled slightly, "will you come visit me?"

Tomkin paused. An image of a little fort nestled in the pine forests of the Scale Mountains came to his mind, smoke rising from a chimney. He wanted to ask if he could come to stay. He shoved that thought away. There was no point in thinking a future that wouldn't happen. "That would be great." It wasn't hard to make that sound sincere.

The torchlight behind Tomkin reflected off a little grin on her face. "I hope your dad finds you a better wife than me."

"Shouldn't be too hard," he answered. "We'll just give her a quick test. Question one. If you were to come into contact with a vicious dragon would you run away, or domesticate it?"

She let out a little giggle.

"Question two. Do you boss people around incessantly? Question three. Have you alienated everyone of importance in the royal court?"

She let out a laugh that was so free and happy Tomkin felt a stab of pain in his chest that he would never hear it again.

"Good luck with that," she said. She started to pull her hand away but Tomkin held it back.

"I don't think it's likely that he'll be able to find someone better."

Her smile faded and she peered up at him.

"But I hope you find what you're looking for." Her hand trembled and he realized she was standing there soaking wet. He dropped her hand. "You should go."

"Don't tell me what to do," she said, but it sounded more habitual than annoyed. She pulled her hand out of the window. "Goodbye, Tomkin. Stop dawdling and go fix the winch."

"Bye, Mags."

There was a rustling noise outside and Tomkin saw a dark shape move across the grass. In a few breaths she had escaped the shadow of the castle and he could see her, running through the moonlight toward the cliff. Tomkin pushed against the wall, straining to see far enough over to watch Lissa begin to climb the path. But in a few more steps, she was out of his view.

Tomkin sank down on the counter and glared at the winch. It couldn't have held a few minutes longer? A few minutes and he'd have been climbing that cliff with Mags right now. He might have even convinced her to come back to Marshwell with him. At least to get Wink.

A few more minutes and the winch could have splintered away and no one would have cared.

"I don't like how my story is being written, Mags," he said to the empty kitchen. He leaned his head back against the wall, exhausted. His limbs were heavy, his back and shoulders ached from fighting the winch. "I always thought I'd play the hero. I never thought I'd be one of those side characters who doesn't even make it back home. Maybe this was your story all along, and I'm just a bit character who helped you through it."

The empty kitchen didn't bother to answer him back. The walls of the castle *were* a prison cell. Every exit was blocked, the wall impenetrable.

Tomkin felt the last of his energy seep out of him, into the stones behind him. The endless rushing of the channel filled the silence. He stared at a torch burning across the room until his eyelids were too heavy to hold open. Then there was nothing but darkness.

CHAPTER TWENTY-ONE

WHEN HE OPENED his eyes again, the kitchen was dark. The chill of the castle wall had seeped into his back, and his stomach felt hollow from hunger. He groaned as he leaned forward and climbed off the counter.

It took him several moments to understand the room was dark because the torches had burned out. His gut clenched and he spun around to look out the window, afraid he would see the sky lightening with dawn. But outside the world was still black. The moon had risen enough that the shadow of the castle where Mags had stood was now full of grass, bleached grey in the moonlight. The moon must have risen high while he slept, but it was hours from dawn.

The only light in the kitchen was the thin flame of the oil lamp. Tomkin found another torch on the shelf by the door and lit it.

He walked back to the winch. The wheel had broken in half and hung off the wall, connected only by a thin splinter of wood. Behind it, the spool that had held the chain was bare. He held the torch up and looked into the hole where the chain had disappeared, but saw nothing.

He hadn't expected to, really.

The kitchen felt distant. His arm holding the torch did so lifelessly. There was no point avoiding the truth of his situation any longer. There was no way out of this castle, and at dawn, Vorath was going to kill him.

He grabbed the dangling piece of wheel and tore it off the wall. It made a satisfying crunch. He grabbed the other side and pulled. The wheel complained with a long groan, but held firm. Tomkin yanked at it. The winch ignored him.

Why wouldn't the stupid thing move?

He yanked again and again. It was broken and useless. And he still couldn't budge it.

He put a foot on the wall and pulled with every bit of strength left in him. He hated this wood more than he had ever hated anything else in his life. His back ached and his hands felt raw. A fury grew inside his chest, until it clawed its way out into a barbaric, enraged roar. The sound filled the kitchen, drowning out, for a breath, the endless rushing of the water.

But the wood did not move. Tomkin shoved himself away from it, panting.

This was not how his story was going to end. He was not going to be devoured by a dragon as an example to his family. He was not going to be the one who hid in the kitchen and scrambled away like a mouse.

Tomkin stood and glared at the kitchen door.

This dragon was going to leave.

Tomkin picked up his sword from the end of the counter and leaned it against his shoulder. Taking a deep breath, he let his anger shove down the fear that was rising, and marched toward the kitchen door.

When he reached the door he glanced back at the dark kitchen. The noise of the channel continued, uncaring. The copper pot must be pressed against the grate by the flow. The water pushing against it relentlessly, sliding by, slipping through the grate, rushing across the kitchen canal and then shooing out into the blackness of the night, before falling, falling, falling through the blackness to smash against the rocks and the river below.

It pulled at him. His mind kept being caught by the water and rushing out into the darkness.

If he were going to be killed and dropped, the channel would do a kinder job than the dragon. He let his hand fall off the kitchen door. It would be so easy. It would only require one step of bravery, and the water would do the rest.

His body ached with exhaustion. He was bruised from being hit by failure after failure. He had been a fool to come here in the first place, and more of a fool for not running at the first glimpse of scales. Running to find someone competent and strong.

The water called to him, but he pictured his broken body, swirling in the bend of the river where his boat had been. He straightened.

His death would not be that useless.

If Vorath killed him this morning, so be it. But if there were only a handful of choices left in his story, Tomkin was going to make them count.

He turned his back resolutely on the water and considered his situation again.

He couldn't fight the dragon. Tomkin didn't have the skills and Vorath had no weaknesses.

He couldn't bargain with the dragon. There was nothing Vorath wanted that Tomkin could leverage. He wanted nothing but revenge. And the only way for him to get it was for Tomkin to die.

What else did the creature want?

The answer flashed into his mind like a white, wooly thing falling from the sky.

Sheep. The dragon wanted sheep and didn't like their wool.

The Isle of Bald Sheep! Tomkin pulled up the memory of

the map he'd looked at back at the holding. It felt like an eternity ago. But it was an entire island overrun with sheep no one wanted. No one except a dragon who didn't like the taste of wool with his mutton.

There were no people nearby. It was the perfect place for a dragon.

Tomkin pushed the kitchen door open and walked into the dark hallway leading to the great hall. The hallway was longer than he remembered it, and colder. Shadows sat defiantly along the edges of the ceiling and near the sunken frames of the doors. The pressure of the emptiness pushed against him. Pushing aside his plan as though it were an insubstantial thing.

Which it was.

He paused. There was no Mags to point out that this plan was just as bad, if not worse, than his original one. How was he going to get a dragon to leave the place he'd wanted his whole life and live on a deserted island?

Tomkin's mind cast about for a better plan, but there was nothing. He straightened his shoulders and raised the torch, sending the ceiling shadows scurrying away for cover.

He wasn't going to let his story end hiding in a hallway.

He strode toward the door to the great hall, purposefully making his footsteps ring. With a yank he pulled the door open, expecting resistance. The hinges gave almost no protest at all and the door swung in, crashing against the wall.

Tomkin flinched and froze as the sound echoed in the great hall.

Nothing stirred in the darkness.

You cannot cower in the servants' hall after slamming the door open. The dragon's voice rang out in his mind, somehow managing to echo, even though Tomkin knew it was only in his mind.

Tomkin took a deep breath and stepped out into the room.

The fires had burned out and the room was terribly dark.

Tomkin's torch lit a small circle of the floor at his feet, but barely reached to the nearest wall. The only other light in the room came from the moonlight dropping in through the gaping windows, outlining just the mound of the dragon's back in flashes of pale light. The rest of the creature was sunken in blackness.

Tomkin gripped the torch and stepped closer until the head of the dragon, resting on the floor, came into view. Unlike the moonlight, the torchlight set the dragon's scales dancing with glints of flaming orange.

Vorath's yellow eyes glittered.

Tomkin swallowed in an effort to banish the dryness in his mouth. His tongue felt huge and ill-formed.

"I've come with an offer." Tomkin's voice was thin in the darkness, not even reaching the walls to echo off.

You have nothing I desire, beyond your life.

"You want sheep," Tomkin pointed out, "and you don't like them wooly."

The dragon looked at him with his flat reptilian eyes.

This wasn't going to work. Vorath didn't want to live on an island in isolation. Tomkin clamped down on his thoughts, trying to keep them as quiet as possible so Vorath couldn't hear them. Tomkin's hand holding the torch shook, making the shadows shudder and the glimmers of light dance over Vorath's scales. Tomkin forced the next words out.

"There's an island south of here. Past Coastal Baylon a half day's row out to sea."

Vorath's eyes stayed fixed on Tomkin and he tried not to shift under the gaze. "It's not a small island, it's quite big. It's named—" He couldn't call it the Isle of Bald Sheep. "It doesn't have a name, but Marshwell owns it, so we'll name it anything you'd like. The Island of Fire and Death? The Dread Isle?"

Vorath didn't move, so Tomkin's mouth hurried to fill the silence.

"It's perfect for you. It's covered with sheep that grow no wool. A few people have tried to domesticate them, to bring them to Marshwell and start a herd, but a bald sheep is only half as valuable as a regular one, so...really the sheep just live there undisturbed. And there are thousands of them."

Vorath was so still that Tomkin had the fleeting, irrational fear the creature had died. Which should have been a good thought, but instead, the idea of the dragon being only paces from him and dead made him feel as though it had been killed by long fingers of shadows, and surely they were coming for Tomkin next.

"There's a volcano at one end," Tomkin said to break the silence, "which is bound to have caves."

The eyes did not blink.

"Volcano caves are warm," he said weakly. "And that sounds...dragony."

Silence stretched through the room. The weight of the dragon's gaze settled on Tomkin until his body felt all gangly and unorganized. He shifted, trying to stand taller, and the movement of the torch sent ripples of light across Vorath's scales. And amidst all the movement of the light, the dragon was perfectly still.

Finally he blinked a long, bored blink.

You want me to leave this castle, the castle I have desired since I was young, leave my revenge on your family untaken, and exile myself to an island in the sea?

Tomkin's throat felt awkward, as though he had no idea how to swallow. He nodded. The movement felt jerky.

Why would I do this?

A flicker of irritation flashed in Tomkin's chest. It was a good idea. Just because the dragon was so consumed with vengeance that he couldn't see it, Tomkin shouldn't have to suffer.

"Because I would like to stay uneaten," Tomkin snapped. "And I'm offering you a way to live in peace." He gestured around the great hall. "To not end up with the same fate as your mother."

The dragon's eyes narrowed to slits and a hiss of hot air blew out of his nostrils. Tomkin smelled hot metal as the breath washed over him. But, as though his chest had turned into some sort of forge, the air fanned his irritation into something stronger.

"Do you really think men will leave you alone here? Do you think you can destroy Marshwell and the rest of the land will just let that pass? More and more men will come. Warriors, knights, assassins, armies." Tomkin took a step forward. "If you kill me, you will begin a series of events that will leave you hunted until you are destroyed. You may be powerful. You may have scales of iron that protect you. But there is only one of you and there are thousands and thousands and thousands of us. And we will make it our goal to destroy you."

Vorath's eyes flashed. *People do not frighten me.*

"Did people frighten your mother?" Tomkin threw back at the dragon, wanting to see Vorath as angry as he was. "Because they should have. And they should frighten you."

The voice was back, the bearded one in Tomkin's head, begging him to stop talking. To consider what he was saying. To consider the fact that he was baiting a dragon who already intended to kill him.

Most of his mind was filled with the terror at what was about to happen, but there was also a thick, deep anger. Anger at everyone who had thought Tomkin incapable of difficult things. Anger at the fact that he was small and good at bargains instead of huge and good at wielding a sword. Anger at this dragon for not having the flaw that he should have. For forcing Tomkin to fail—and die failing.

"You may be able to defeat me, but you won't defeat them all. Someone will get past your fire and past your scales, and you will die, alone, in a gully in the mountains."

Vorath lifted his head until Tomkin had to crane his neck up to meet the monster's furious gaze. Behind the creature light seeped over the eastern horizon, washing out the stars and dropping the land into a shadow that felt darker than the night.

The dragon's silhouette hung between Tomkin and the dawn. Air sucked past Tomkin as the dragon drew in a breath, and Tomkin knew the fire was coming.

Tomkin thought of Mags running toward the Scale Mountains. At least he had rescued the girl. Not that anyone was going to know. Mags wasn't going to stop by the holding to let them know.

No, if Tomkin were remembered at all, it would only be as the first death among many.

Tomkin saw the nostrils flare. Gripping his Granduncle's sword, as though it would do anything against the coming destruction, he pulled his mind away from the approaching fire and closed his eyes

He pictured Mags, getting farther and farther away from this place every moment. He let his mind run there with her, far away from this moment, from the coming fire.

Run, Mags, he thought, willing any small bit of energy he had left to her.

"If you burn that boy," Mags' imperious voice came cutting through the great hall, "I will destroy this castle."

Vorath's gaze snapped to the back of the room and Tomkin spun around.

There, glaring at the dragon and dirtier than ever, stood Mags.

CHAPTER TWENTY-TWO

TOMKIN STARED AT HER, everything in his body aghast at the sight of her.

"What are you doing here?" Tomkin demanded.

"Saving you." Mags stepped up next to him and gave him a prim smile. "You're welcome. I ran into Wink coming back because he didn't want to leave me here, and we decided you would probably need help. Obviously, we were right."

"What is wrong with you?" Tomkin demanded. "I got you out! You were free! All you had to do was run and do something sensible for once!"

Mags turned to him, her eyes furious. "You knew," she hissed at him. "You knew you couldn't fix the winch."

"You were free." Tomkin stared at her, his mind slamming against the question of how she could be back.

There was fury in her face, but also pain and confusion and more emotions than Tomkin could hope to sort out. "You lied to me."

Something snapped inside of him. He glared at her and then at Vorath. "Yes, I lied. It was my turn."

Vorath cocked his head and watched the two of them.

"How did you get back in?" Tomkin demanded. "And why are you so filthy again?"

"Because you sent me up a steep, muddy trail!" She put her hands on her hips. "Liar."

"Of course I lied! I wanted you to go. To get away from here and stop putting yourself in danger over a stupid plan to live in this castle, which besides being inhabited by a dragon,"—He flung one arm at the enormous creature in front of him— "belongs to *me*."

"It belongs to your father," Lissa pointed out.

"Why didn't you kill me before she showed up?" Tomkin yelled at Vorath. "At least then I would have died thinking I had saved her useless hide."

"It's not your job to save me." Mags stomped one dirty foot on the floor. "I don't need you to rescue me, or think you know better than me."

Mags turned away from him and stepped toward the dragon. "You"—she leveled a tiny finger at the dragon's enormous snout— "lied to me, too. We had a deal. I help you fix the castle, you and I live here together. But you didn't plan on doing that, did you?"

She was so small standing there, one hand on her hip, glaring at the creature in front of her. Tomkin knew it was coming. The fire was coming and it would burn both of them now. She looked so brave and so foolish standing there.

"You think you're so indestructible because of your big teeth and your shiny scales," she waved a dismissive hand at the dragon's enormous body. "But I've had Wink shrink the foundation stones of this castle. And if you don't give me your word—your actual word that you will honor your promises—I'll have him shrink every stone in this ruin and send the rubble rolling down into the river."

Tomkin stared at Mags. That was a decent bargaining chip. Tomkin glanced around and saw Wink standing near the back of the room.

"And if anything happens to me," Mags continued, "he'll destroy this place."

If you destroy this castle, Vorath's voice was unconcerned, *I will fly out of it and you will fall with it into the river. Then I will go and lay waste to not only Marshwell, I will destroy Greentree as well. I will raze your home and burn your fields. The people of your land will run in terror and I will hunt them down, one by one.*

An image slammed into Tomkin's head of Vorath soaring over a town of people, destroying and burning at will. Weapons would be powerless. Maybe someday, someone would hurt the creature. But until then, he would destroy everything he found.

Swords could not hurt him. Arrows would bounce harmlessly off the orange scales.

The scales.

Tomkin's mind latched on to the idea and he shoved his hand into his pocket. His fingers ran over the tiny ridges on the scale.

There it was. There was the leverage. Nothing as complicated as revenge. Just pure, animal survival.

Trying to ignore the pictures of destruction being shoved at his mind, he motioned for Wink to come closer and held out the scale to him. "Does this have enough iron that you could shrink it?"

The kobold took the scale with two knobby fingers. "Yes, but I'm not wasting energy on something as useless as a single scale."

Tomkin tipped his head toward the dragon. "Is it connected enough to all of those, that you can shrink them all?"

Wink's eyes widened, and a vicious grin flashed across the kobold's face. He reached out and took the scale from Tomkin.

"Not yet," Tomkin whispered.

The images of Vorath destroying things ran in his mind,

but he pushed them aside again. Mags was still standing before the onslaught of the vision, but she was wilting. Tomkin stepped up beside her, placing his shoulder against hers. She was blinking back tears, but at his touch she lifted her chin slightly.

"You're right," Tomkin said loudly, into the silence of the great hall. The sound of it faded the images as Vorath's attention moved to Tomkin. "You're right. You can come to our homes and destroy us and there is very little we can do. We cannot hope to defeat a dragon as well-protected as you."

Vorath's eyes narrowed.

"The way things stand, you would overpower us." Tomkin stepped forward again. "So let's *adjust the scales* a bit, shall we?"

Tomkin looked pointedly at the scales on Vorath's chest.

Nothing happened. The scales remained, rising and falling with the dragon's breath, perfect and impenetrable.

Tomkin glanced behind him at Wink. The kobold was holding the dragon's scale between two knobby fingers and spinning it with the other hand.

"Really?" Tomkin demanded. "No story in history has had that good of a setup, and you're not paying attention?"

The kobold looked at him blankly.

"Adjust the scales!" Tomkin hissed at the creature.

Wink scowled at Tomkin before narrowing his eyes at the dragon.

A low growl began deep in the dragon's chest and it fixed an annoyed look at Tomkin. Mags took a half step backwards.

Tomkin focused on the large scales covering the curve of the dragon's chest.

They began to shrink.

The scale he was watching drew back, growing smaller, separating from the ones next to it. A sliver of white flesh appeared at the edge of it.

Vorath twisted and snapped his jaw at his chest as every

scale shrank, revealing thin snakes of white flesh, which gradually grew until each scale was surrounded by exposed skin.

Vorath roared, twisting and thrashing.

STOP! The dragon's voice crashed into Tomkin's mind, dropping him to his knees. Beside him he heard Mags cry out.

Tomkin met Wink's questioning gaze and nodded. The scales on the dragon stopped shrinking.

Vorath sat curled up, backed up against the wall, his body coiled to attack. He let out a long, vicious hiss.

Tomkin stood slowly, warily. Vorath's eyes followed the movement, burning with hatred. The creature began to draw in a deep breath.

"If anything happens to us," Tomkin said quickly, "Wink will shrink every scale off your body."

Next to him, Wink blinked invisible.

"He has your scale, and you see what he can do...."

Vorath held his breath for a moment. When he let it out, there was no fire, but scorching hot air rushed into Tomkin's face, and he ducked his face away from it.

"Your scales will grow back," Tomkin said when it stopped. "Right, Wink?"

Wink's voice came out of the darkness. "There's nothing wrong with them, they're just smaller."

Tomkin nodded. "But now, if you go to Marshwell or Greentree, you won't overpower us. Instead of a million impenetrable scales, you have a million chinks in your armor. Every arrow, every sword, every spear will have a million targets.

"You may destroy some of us, but you will destroy yourself as well."

Vorath clenched his claws, scraping deep grooves into the flagstones. He threw his head back and let out a roar that shook the castle. Tomkin stumbled back into Mags, who grabbed his arm.

"I've given you a good option," Tomkin said. "The island

is a good place. It gives you what you want, it gives us what we want. You go to a land you can rule without contest, a place providing everything you need. And we get to live and not have our homes destroyed." He thrust an image of a map to the island at the dragon, as loudly as his thoughts could manage.

Vorath's head came down until his jaw hung right in front of Tomkin, his fangs within easy reach.

Tomkin forced himself to stand still, forced himself not to back away from the nostrils that were covered now in pallid skin with a sparse scattering of tiny scales across it. The skin looked raw and exposed.

I will destroy you.

"I don't think so," Tomkin said, holding Vorath's gaze and forcing his words to sound brave. "Wink is going to keep your scale. If you decide that revenge would taste better than bald sheep, the kobold will shrink your scales until they disappear altogether." He stared at one tiny, perfect scale at the end of Vorath's nose, surrounded by white skin. "I'm not positive, but I think there's a fair chance that if he does, the scales will not grow back."

A deep growl rumbled in Vorath's chest. Tomkin fought to not back away.

Mags stepped up next to Tomkin. "It's time you left, Vorath. If we hear you are anywhere in Queensland, we will come find you."

The dragon's gaze flicked between the two of them. Tomkin reached over and gripped Mags' hand. It was shaking, but she stood tall.

Air sucked past Tomkin into the dragon. Vorath lifted his head and his wings unfurled. A noise like thundering water rushed out of the monster. Tomkin dropped the sword and grabbed Mags, pulling her to the floor as a river of flame shot out above them.

Vorath thrashed his head around, spraying fire across the

room. Tomkin ducked behind his arm and watched the flames above him until the heat became unbearable, and he pushed himself and Mags lower against the floor. The cool stones beneath him shook with the dragon's fury.

Claw scraped against stone and cold air rushed back over him.

Tomkin looked up to see the pale shape of Vorath slithering toward the gaping windows. With a scramble and a scattering of stones, the dragon flung himself out the window, spread his pale orange wings until they blocked the rising sun, then banked south and disappeared down the Great River.

CHAPTER TWENTY-THREE

TOMKIN SCRAMBLED up and ran to the window. The sun was peeking warily over the horizon. Off to the south, winging its way down the Great River, was the light orange dragon.

Tomkin sank back against the side of the window, his body flooding with relief.

"It worked!" Mags leaned out the window and watched Vorath disappear into the dim morning light. She turned to Tomkin. "That was brilliant! Absolutely brilliant!"

Tomkin grinned at her. "I can't believe you were going to make the castle fall off the cliff!" He looked around quickly. "It's not going to, is it?"

Mags shook her head, her own grin wide. "Saying Wink shrank some of the stones might have been a slight exaggeration. He did figure out which ones he would need to shrink, should it be necessary."

Tomkin laughed. "Again with the lies." He turned to look at the brightening world. Morning light set the tops of the hills afire with glowing green grass and left the valleys drenched in darkness. Cool air swirled in the windows, smelling fresh with the newness of the day. He felt light enough to float into the sky.

"It's beautiful," Mags said, standing next to him.

Tomkin hesitated a moment, then put his arm around her shoulders.

She grabbed his hand and looked up at him, concerned. "Are you still dizzy?"

"Um…no." He looked at her from the corner of his eye. "Is that okay?"

She tensed under his arm and he began to draw it back, but she held on to his hand.

"It's okay." She looked back at the sunrise.

Tomkin tried to relax his arm, but it didn't seem to be listening to him.

She gave a little shrug. "It's not surprising that even without a head injury, you still need help standing."

Tomkin snorted a little laugh. Mags slid her arm around his waist and leaned her head on his shoulder. She felt so small beneath his arm, but so steady.

"You're a very solid girl," he said.

She flashed a smile at him.

"…when you're not being delusional."

She nudged his leg with her hip. "You're quite brave. For a boy who's dim."

Tomkin looked out over the hills to the east. The birds across the river were singing their tiny hearts out as though this were the first morning on earth. He could stand here forever.

Except moments never did last forever. He was exhausted, and hungry, and at some point they would need to leave this window and…

"Lissa," Tomkin said finally, "I understand why you left Greentree. If you don't want me to tell them you've gone to the Scale Mountains, I won't. I'll find a way to call off the agreement our parents made." He glanced at her. "It's got to be easier to end an engagement than to chase off a dragon."

"You would think," she said, still looking out the window.

He felt the rise and fall of her shoulders beneath his arm. "But someday, when you feel comfortable returning, will you come find me? I'm going to see if I can convince my father to let me rebuild this castle and live here. It's close enough to the holding that I can get there easily to help, and most of the work I do for him is paperwork anyway. Which I can do from here...."

She was quiet for a long time.

Tomkin swallowed. "I understand if you don't want to think about coming back."

She shook her head and looked at him. "I'm not going to the Scales," she said at last. "It's time my father and I talked."

Tomkin felt his heart beat a little faster, and hoped she couldn't feel it too.

"And...," She paused for a long moment. "...maybe we shouldn't end the engagement quite yet."

He tried to keep his arm perfectly still. It felt weirdly wooden. "No?"

She shrugged again. "I had always hoped to marry an intelligent man, but I think you might have some good qualities. Hiding deep, deep inside of you."

Tomkin smiled. "You want to marry me."

"Maybe. Someday in the far future. I'm certainly not ready to marry you today—"

"That's good, because you're far too dirty for a wedding."

She laughed and continued as though he hadn't spoken. "—but maybe we should leave the agreement in place for a bit. At least take some time to hammer out the details of it. Like the fact that we would have to be given this castle. And how Wink would come with me instead of staying with my family." She looked up at him, biting her lip. "Unless you'd still rather fight a dragon than marry me?"

Tomkin snorted. "Sweet heavens, no! It turns out fighting a dragon is hard. And terrifying. Even more terrifying than you."

She smiled. "You're going to miss having a dragon around, aren't you?"

Tomkin squeezed her shoulder. "I think I still do."

She jabbed her shoulder into his side. "Let's get out of here. Wink made a little doorway in the castle wall near the lake. We can get out there."

Tomkin looked at her. "He made a doorway. In the castle wall."

She bit her lip and nodded.

"How long did that take him?"

A little smile crept across her face. "A few minutes."

He stared at her for a long moment. "That would have been useful last night."

A giggle escaped her before she clamped her lips shut. She nodded. "I know."

The laugh that rose in Tomkin grew, eating up all the terror of the night, until it burst out and echoed throughout the great hall, mingling with Mags'. Tomkin turned them away from the window. Picking up Scalebreaker and still laughing, the two headed toward the stairs that would lead them out.

From the bailey, Tomkin could see the small archway cut through the castle wall. It only came up to his waist, but through it he could see the grass outside. "Wink's going to need to make the back door a lot bigger."

Mags rolled her eyes. "You're welcome."

She knelt to crawl through.

"Mags," he said, and she paused. "I know Greentree is not the same direction as Marshwell from here. But if you wanted to come to Marshwell with me first, we could...find some horses. And I could ride with you to Greentree...as some sort of escort or something."

She raised one eyebrow at him.

"To make sure you don't move in with any dragons you find along the way."

169

She laughed. "As long as you don't bring a sword."

"Agreed. And maybe after that we can take a trip to Queenstown. I've never been to court, but I hear Princess Ellona hasn't been treating my future wife very well."

Mags rolled her eyes. "Yes, I'm sure a stern talking-to from you will fix things." She turned and crawled out of the castle.

"I defeated a dragon!" Tomkin called out through the arch.

Mags' laugh came back in. "You denuded a dragon."

"Are you saying that's what I should try with the princess?"

"Will you come on?" Mags said, still laughing that bright laugh. "You've been trying to get out of this castle all night. What's the holdup?"

Tomkin looked around at the bailey and the keep and the stairs to the great hall. Amidst the morning light and the echoes of laughter, the ruins felt alive with possibilities. He thought of Mags' drawing. Yes, Colbreth Castle would be perfect.

What better place was there for two dragon conquerors to live out their days?

THE EVER AFTER

LULU GAZED up at Keeper Will from where she sat at his feet. His voice had stopped, and beside the crackle of the fire, the quiet hung in the air of the inn like a living thing. She couldn't bear to break the silence, but the question burst out anyway.

"Did they live happy, to the end of their days?"

Will smiled at her. "Castle Colbreth, with the help of Wink, was turned into one of the finest castles in the land. Tomkin Thornhewn made his home there, along with his wife, Lady Lissa of Marshwell."

A spattering of cheers echoed in the common room.

"They visited the royal court two times."

"The first time, Tomkin was knighted for his valor in defense of the realm. Back in those days, there was nothing similar to knighting for women, but Tomkin negotiated with the king, until His Majesty bestowed upon Mags the title of Lady Lissa, The Dragon Charmer.

"A title which Tomkin was fond of shortening to The Dragon."

He waited until the clapping and cheers died down.

"The details of Tomkin's negotiations with the king were

never publicly released. But less than a year later, Tomkin and The Dragon visited Queenstown for their second trip. This time to witness the marriage of Princess Ellona to the elderly, malodorous King of Coastal Baylon, sealing a treaty of peace between the two lands."

Will paused again for hoots of approval. He looked down at Lulu with a thoughtful expression.

"I cannot say, Lulu, that Tomkin and The Dragon lived happily to the end of their days, because happiness is trickier than that. They had plenty of hard days, and plenty of sad days, but they did try to be kind to each other. And kindness takes you a long way on the path to happiness. So I think it is safe to say Tomkin and The Dragon lived, on the balance, happy-ish to the end of their days."

The inn erupted in cheers. Keeper Will bowed his head in acknowledgement.

Lulu looked at the flower in her fingers. Flashes of orange scales danced in her mind—the huge, fiery dragon, Tomkin and Lissa standing tall before it. The magic of the flower and the magic of the story swirled together, catching her up and twirling her thoughts around.

Keeper Will leaned forward and asked in a confidential voice, "What did you think of my story?"

"I loved it." Lulu grinned up at him. "Will you tell it again?"

THE END

AFTERWORD

Thank you for reading *A Keeper's Tale: The Story of Tomkin and the Dragon*. I hope it was as fun to read as it was to write. If you enjoyed it and have the time to leave a review, I would appreciate it.

A review is worth more to an author than an entire army of warriors would have been to Tomkin around chapter 18.

If you have the time to leave a review, you can click here.

Read more about the Keepers and their stories in *The Keeper Chronicles*.

The series begins with *A Threat of Shadows*. You can find it and other books of mine on my website at jaandrews.com.

You can read chapter one of *A Threat of Shadows* at the end of this book.

A THREAT OF SHADOWS

THE KEEPER
CHRONICLES
BOOK I

If you'd like a quick note when I have new releases out, please sign up for my Bookish Things newsletter. I send short emails a few times a month letting you know about anything new in my own books and any good sales or promotions I come across.

If you're a social media fan you can find me on Facebook and Twitter.

(Turn to the next page to read chapter one of A Threat of Shadows.)

A THREAT OF SHADOWS - CH 1

THE DEEPER ALARIC rode into the woods, the more something felt... off. This forest had always fit like a well-worn cloak. But tonight, the way the forest wrapped around felt familiar, but not quite comfortable, as though it remembered wrapping around a slightly different shape.

"This path used to be easier to follow," Alaric said to his horse, Beast, as they paused between patches of summer moonlight. Alaric peered ahead, looking for the trail leading to the Stronghold. He found it running like a scratch through the low brush to the right. "If the Keepers weren't too meek to hold grudges, I'd think the old men were hiding it from me."

All the usual smells of pine and moss and dirt wove through the air, the usual sounds of little animals going about their lives, but Alaric kept catching a hint of something different. Something more complicated than he wanted to deal with.

Around the next turn, the trail ran straight into a wide tree trunk. Alaric leaned as far to the side as he could, but he couldn't see around it. "I could be wrong about the Keepers holding grudges."

Well, if they didn't want him at the Stronghold, that was

too bad. He didn't need a warm welcome. He just needed to find one book with one antidote. With a little luck, the book would be easy to find and he could leave quickly. With a lot of luck, he'd get in and out without having to answer anyone's questions about what he'd been doing for the past year.

Beast circled the tree and found the path again, snaking out the other side. As his hooves thudded down on it, a howl echoed through the woods.

The horse froze, and Alaric grabbed the pouch hanging around his neck, protecting it against his chest. He closed his eyes, casting out past the nearest trees and through the woods, searching for the blazing energy of the wolf. He sensed nothing beyond the tranquil glow of the trees and the dashing flashes of frightened rabbits.

"That's new." Alaric opened his eyes and peered into the darkness.

A louder howl broke through the night. Beast shuddered.

"It's all right." Alaric patted Beast's neck as he cast farther out. The life energy of an animal as large as a wolf would be like a bonfire among the trees, but there was nothing near them. "It's not wolves. Just disembodied howls." He kept his voice soothing, hoping to calm the animal.

"That didn't sound as reassuring as I meant it to. But a real wolf pack wouldn't keep howling as they got closer. If we were being tracked by wolves, we wouldn't know it."

Beast's ears flicked back and forth, alert for another howl.

"Okay, that wasn't reassuring, either." Alaric nudged him forward. "C'mon we're almost to the Wall."

A third howl tore out of the darkness right beside them.

Beast reared back, whinnying in terror. Alaric grabbed for the saddle and swore. He pressed his hand to Beast's neck.

"*Paxa*," he said, focusing energy through his hand and into Beast. A shock of pain raced across Alaric's palm where it touched the horse, as the energy rushed through.

Mid-snort, Beast settled and stood still.

Alaric shook out his hand and looked thoughtfully into the woods. This wasn't about a grudge, or at least the howls weren't directed at him. Any Keeper would know there were no wolves. Even one as inadequate as he would know there was no energy, no *vitalle*, behind the sounds. So what was the purpose of it? The path had never been like this before.

With Beast calm, Alaric set him back into a steady walk. Two more howls rang out from the woods, but Beast ambled along, unruffled. Alaric rubbed his still-tingling palm.

Beast paused again as the trail ran into another wide tree.

Alaric growled in frustration. The path to the Keepers' Stronghold shouldn't be this troublesome for a Keeper.

Unless it no longer recognized him as one. That was a sobering thought.

As they skirted around the tree, a white face thrust itself out of the trunk. Alaric jerked away as the hazy form of a man leaned out toward him. When the figure didn't move, Alaric reined in Beast and forced himself to study it. It held no life energy, it was just an illusion—like the wolves.

The figure was a young man. He had faded yellow hair and milky white skin. Once the initial shock wore off, the man was not particularly frightening.

"What are you supposed be? A friendly ghost?" Alaric asked.

It hung silent on the tree. Alaric leaned forward and backward, but the ghost remained still, staring off into the woods.

"The howls were more frightening than you." Alaric set Beast to walking again.

"You are lost," the ghost whispered as he passed.

Alaric gave a short laugh. "I've been lost many times in my life, but this isn't one of them. And if it's your job to scare people off, you should consider saying something more chilling and less...depressing."

Beast kept walking, and Alaric turned to watch the ghost fade into the darkness behind them.

A rasp pulled his attention forward. Another white form slid out of the tree they were approaching. This one was a young woman. She was rather pretty, for a ghost.

"Hello." Alaric gave her a polite nod.

"You have failed," she whispered. "You have failed everyone."

Alaric scowled. The words rang uncomfortably true.

Alaric stopped Beast in front of the ghost. Behind the woman's face, Alaric saw thin, silver runes carved on the bark. He couldn't read them through the ghost, but he didn't need to. Narrowing his focus, he cast out ahead of them along the trail, brushing against the trunks with his senses. Now that he knew what he was looking for, he felt the subtle humming runes dotting the trees ahead.

Alaric sat back in the saddle. This wasn't what he expected from the Keepers. The old men protected their privacy like paranoid hermits, but they'd never tried to scare people away before. Of course, these ghosts weren't frightening. If the Keepers were going to make ghosts, these are the kind they would make.

Years ago, during his "Defeat by Demoralization" lesson, Keeper Gerone had declared, "Control the emotions, control the man!" Gerone was probably responsible for the depressing ghosts.

The ghost runes were on almost every tree now, faces appearing every few steps.

"Your powers are worthless," the next whispered and Alaric flinched.

"It's your fault," another rasped. "All your fault."

Alaric clenched his jaw and stared ahead as the whispers surrounded him.

When he passed close to one large tree, a ghost thrust out close to him. Alaric turned toward it and saw his own face

178

looking back at him. A pale, wasted version of himself. His black hair was faded to a lifeless grey, and his skin, far from being tanned from traveling, was bleached a wrinkly bone white. Only his eyes had stayed dark, sinking from a healthy brown to deep, black pits.

Alaric stared, repulsed, at the withered apparition of himself—it was decades older than his forty years. The ghost looked tired, a deep crease furrowed between its brows. Alaric reached up and rubbed his own forehead.

The ghost leaned closer.

"She's dead," it whispered.

Guilt stabbed into him, deep and familiar. He shuddered, grabbing the pouch at his neck, his mind flooded with the image of Evangeline's sunken face.

Alaric slammed his palm against the rune on the trunk.

"*Uro!*" Pain raced through his hand again. He poured energy into the tree, willing it to burn. The bark smoked as he seared the rune off.

Out of the corner of his eye, pulses of white light appeared along the path ahead of them. He glanced at them, but the distraction had consequences, and the pain flared, arcing up each finger. He gasped and narrowed his focus back to the energy flowing through his palm. The pain receded slightly. The ghost stared a moment longer, then faded away. Alaric dropped his arm, leaving a hand-shaped scorch mark on the trunk where the rune had been.

"She's dead."

Alaric's head snapped forward.

The trees ahead of him were full of ghosts, each a washed-out version of himself.

"Dead... She's dead... Dead." The words filled the air.

Alaric clutched the pouch at his neck until he felt the rough stone inside.

A ghost reached toward him. "She's dead..." Its voice rattled in a long sigh.

Alaric spurred Beast into a gallop, trusting the horse to follow the trail. The whispers clung to them as they ran. Alaric shrank down, hunching his shoulders, wresting his mind away from the memory of his wife's tired eyes, her pale skin.

The trees ended, and they raced out into a silent swath of grass, running up to the base of an immense cliff. Alaric pulled Beast to a stop, both of them breathing hard. Gripping the saddle, Alaric looked back into the trees. The forest was dark and quiet.

"I take it back," he said, catching his breath, "the ghosts were worse than the wolves." He sat in the saddle, pushing back the dread that was enveloping him. She wasn't dead. The ghosts were just illusions. He'd get the antidote tonight. She'd be fine.

When his heart finally slowed, he gave Beast an exhausted pat on the neck.

"This path used to be a *lot* easier to follow."

(If you'd like to continue reading A Threat of Shadows, you can find it here.)

RECOMMENDED READING

Uncommon World
By Alisha Klapheke

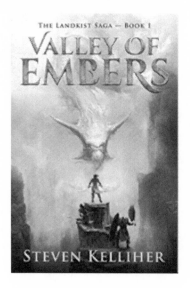

Valley of Embers
By Steven Kelliher

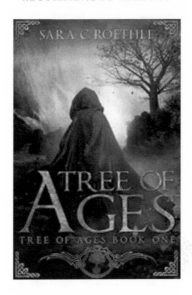

Tree of Ages
By Sara Roethle

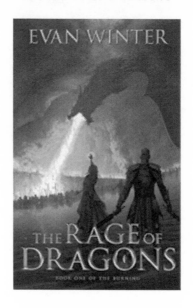

The Rage of Dragons
By Evan Winter

Her Dangerous Visions
By Brandon Barr

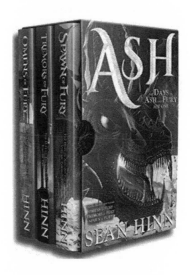

The Days of Ash and Fury (Trilogy)
By Sean Hinn

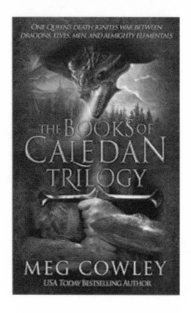

The Books of Caledan Trilogy
By Meg Cowley

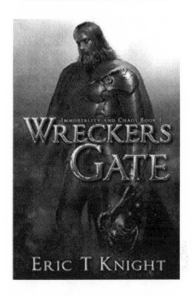

Wreckers Gate
By Eric T. Knight

The Dragon Songs Saga
By JC Kang

Darkmage
By M.L. Spencer

The Five Warriors (Four Worlds Series Book 1)
By Angela J. Ford

ACKNOWLEDGMENTS

Thank you to Cheryl (again) for all your help, it, has been invaluable.

To the Fantasy Faction, thank you for the excellent critiques and the camaraderie. Special thanks to Sherry Bessette, Joey Harpel, Caroline Sciriha, and Nick Wisseman for all your input.

Thank you to CJ Brightley and Jacky Gray for your comments and encouragement.

Thank you to Christos Karapanos at www.christoskara-panos.com for the gorgeous dragon eye on the cover. And thank you to Dane at ebooklaunch.com for the beautiful cover design.

To my awesome children, thank you for helping Tomkin plan a way out of the kitchen.

And most of all, thank you to my husband, who after 18 years is still my favorite person. Your support and encouragement mean more to me than you'll probably ever know. I love you and the fun, happy life you've made for our family.

ABOUT THE AUTHOR

JA Andrews is a writer, wife, mother, and unemployed rocket scientist. She doesn't regret the rocket science degree, but finds it generally inapplicable in daily life. Except for the rare occurrence of her being able to definitively state, "That's not rocket science." She does, however, love the stars.

She spends an inordinate amount of time at home, with her family, who she adores, and lives deep in the Rocky Mountains of Montana, where she can see more stars than she ever imagined.

For more information, find JA Andrews at:
www.jaandrews.com
jaandrews@jaandrews.com

Made in the USA
Las Vegas, NV
26 August 2021